Dictates demanded Simon be the judge, and Martha the accused....

Martha was entitled to a fair trial regardless, and Simon would see that she had one. Professionalism, to the bitter end. This was, after all, his stock in trade. Ironic. He looked again at the painting of the broken craft going down, and knew how it felt to be lost at sea. He was not at his professional best, but vulnerable somehow. Again, the irony struck him. How could he be the strong one, in control, if he was this vulnerable?

GRACE'S PRIVATE
SANCTUARY

A MYSTERY

VIRGINIA DeMASI

SOUL'S
ROAD
PRESS

GRACE'S PRIVATE SANCTUARY
Virginia DeMasi

Print edition published 2015 by Soul's Road Press

First Edition

ISBN-13: 978-0692469521 (trade paperback)
ISBN-10: 0692469524 (trade paperback)

Inquiries should be addressed to
Soul's Road Press
info@soulsroadpress.com
http://www.soulsroadpress.com

Cover image © EarthCapture / Bigstock.com
Soul's Road Press logo © Designs by Trapdoor

Dedication

To John and David for all of your love and support.
And to my Aunt Annette, the inspiration for this story.
Yours is the kindest heart; the gentlest soul.

All my love.
—Ginny

GRACE'S PRIVATE
SANCTUARY

A MYSTERY

Chapter 1

DOCTOR SIMON TALBOT rubbed his tired eyes, and glanced at the walls covered with diplomas and the priceless oils paintings of sinking ships. He thought soberly that his life was there in the art.

Outside his office window, he could barely see the capitol building of Albany. The beautiful Dutch architecture looked precious and grand no matter how dreary the weather. He wished he could transport himself back to the time when the settlers executed plans and erected structures so solid, they were still intact today.

He forced himself to tear himself away, sit at his desk, and open the file of Mrs. Henning. Martha Reed's handwriting jumped out at him. The neat script made his stomach churn, his pulse quicken. Unsettling, half-forgotten memories crept forward, and he made an effort to focus on the pages. The report described a normal physical exam. Martha had supported her conclusions with a battery of tests. So far, so good.

Simon flipped the ecru sheet of paper with its official seal and the imprint of the Medical Society. He placed tortoise-rimmed bifocals on the bridge of his nose and brought the document closer to his face. It was the same no matter what angle he held it, no matter the room in which he sat. Said the same thing. Made the same charge. The grievance had been filed by the county board of medical examiners—the Medical Society—several weeks ago. It argued that Doctor Reed was negligent.

It seemed the big boys were bending over backwards to police themselves, afraid that otherwise, the public might do it for them. A clerk reviewing records did a random check on facility fatalities, and Martha Reed had just gotten lucky. Supposedly.

Martha was in up to her neck, if instinct served him. It gave him a bitter taste. He knew he wasn't going into this with an open mind. He was biased, and he hated that.

Dictates demanded he be the judge, and she the accused. She was entitled to a fair trial regardless, and he'd see that she had one. Professionalism, to the bitter end. This was, after all, his stock in trade. Ironic. He looked again at the painting of the broken craft going down, and knew how it felt to be lost at sea. He was not at his professional best, but vulnerable somehow. Again, the irony struck him. How could he be the strong one, in control, if he was this vulnerable?

A moment later the door swung wide, and the threshold was clouded by a figure with lustrous dark hair and the luminous green eyes he remembered too well.

"Martha."

"Simon."

He welcomed her with a warm handshake and gestured for her to sit in his favorite chair, opposite his desk. His refuge might well become her own.

"Thank you for seeing me on such short notice."

"Well, it's my pleasure, Martha."

He returned to the chair on his side of the desk and noticed how she'd crossed her legs at the knees. A defense mechanism—no, he wouldn't allow himself to digress into that. Not with Martha. He leaned back, discovered he had hunkered down as if expecting a battle, and asked, "Do you think spring will ever come?"

"It's got to. It's May already."

The grandfather clock stood sentinel, paternally marking the time. Simon waited as she surveyed his room, neck craning with a delicacy reserved for porcelain figurines. What she didn't notice were the dusky gray eyes watching her as she studied the room. It was a gracious room. The walls were lined with solid wood bookcases, filled with medical texts, the occasional classic, and a few pieces of colorful blown glass.

"How long has it been, Martha, five years?"

She shifted in her seat. "Oh, I don't know. Something like that. I don't know…four, maybe."

"Let's see. You were in your second year at medical school. You've since had a year of internship and two years of residency, and you've done well. I've been following your career."

"Have you?"

"I certainly have. You've made me proud."

"Up until now."

"No. I'm still proud." He paused. "It's odd to think you've never written."

She faltered. "I've just been so…busy."

"All that time, Martha?" He knew he should let it go, but couldn't. "Medical conferences over the years, symposiums, lecture series. All that time, you were too busy to look up an old colleague—never a spare minute for your old mentor? I expected you to have contacted me many times by now."

He watched as she looked awkwardly into her lap.

"If I didn't know better, I'd say you've been avoiding me. But it doesn't matter. I scrutinize too much."

"Yes," she said, her voice a whisper.

"Too Freudian for your taste."

"I never believed in Freud," she countered.

He was enjoying this, until the chain mail façade he always wore slipped to his knees and a keen sensation shot through his groin. He tried to ignore it.

"It made you uncomfortable. But you liked Jung."

She considered what he said. "I thought he had a firmer grasp on reality. Now, I'm not so sure. They were close at one time."

He frowned. He tried to concentrate. Goddammit, be professional. This was not what he wanted. More than anything, he wanted justice for her—to do what was right.

"Until their falling out," he heard himself say. "The classic pair. First, comrades in arms then bitter rivals. Sound familiar?"

She looked across at him. "We were never bitter rivals."

He knew he was going to have to work hard to establish the ground rules before it was too late.

"Regardless of whose decree you follow, what we don't know is greater than what we do."

She wasn't listening, staring at the paintings on every wall in the beautiful office. Did she know he'd bought them at a time in his life when he himself had plunged into the depths of despair? And that she was the cause?

"This charge," he broke in to her reverie. "That you hadn't adequately restricted Mrs. Henning's mobility on sanitarium grounds, and that said negligence had resulted directly in the accident—"

"Is all rubbish."

Simon shook his head. "To you, maybe. But it's a serious charge. I'll do my best—"

"To preserve the integrity of the profession? The good old boy network? Won't you, Simon?"

"I'd think twice before I took the high-handed road if I were you, Martha. My judgment here could affect the remainder of your career."

"Yes, it could." She said it as if she didn't care.

Simon stood, took off his white coat, and hung it on the coat rack. It was a symbolic gesture, to remove the distance between them. Of course this would be difficult. How could it not be? He sat down, pulled a pen from his pocket, and scribbled silently across the top of a pad.

"I've heard you've been successful at the Helsey Institute, and I take it you like Saratoga? It was a tremendous coup, you know. Getting that position."

"Yes, and I thank you for it." She stared directly at him. "If I didn't before, I thank you now."

She pulled open a loose-leaf binder that she'd carried with her, clearing her throat. Ready to fight.

Hope rose, and Simon smiled inwardly. Yes, this was his protégé. Now she'd give him a run for his money. He turned in his seat. "So. Let's get down to business."

"I brought enough material to keep us here forever."

Simon gritted his teeth.

"I wish circumstances were different," he began, but thought better of it. "Tell me everything, from the beginning. Don't worry about context."

He knew she was resolved to keep her license. He wondered if he'd be capable of taking it, if it came to that. After all the years of sweat and study, and the forfeiture of any real semblance of life, Simon knew how much that would hurt.

"On January the sixteenth, Grace came to me for the first time," Martha said. "I did the usual exam, and filed the necessary reports, which I have here. Do you want to see them?"

"I'm one step ahead, Martha." He patted the opened file on his desk. "I have your initial reports here."

Martha stared, dazed, at the sheaf of papers on the polished desk.

"Her GP's lab reports showed nothing unusual physically. He requested that causes of dementia be ruled out." Simon cleared his throat. Mercifully, the physician within him took over. "What was determined to be the cause of dementia?"

"No cause, secondary to cerebrovascular disease. There was no alcohol abuse or hydrocephalus. And I dismissed the prospect of head trauma or metabolic conditions."

Simon scribbled furiously. Now they spoke in terms he could negotiate safely. "Go on."

"She took no medications. Remember, she came to me with symptoms of disorientation and confusion."

"Mm-hmm," he prompted, not looking up.

"I was a competent psychiatrist."

"An inexperienced one," he put in.

"All right, that's fine, if that's what you need, Simon."

"Not what I need."

"Yes, you do, if you have to establish the fact that I haven't the years under my belt you have. If you need that on record."

"Martha, this isn't on record. Right now I'm just making some notes to myself." He dropped his pen. "You know, inexperience is not a sin."

"I have associations among the best universities, and I'm well regarded."

"I know that. Don't you think that I, of all people, am aware of your status among your peers? But you can be well respected and inexperienced."

She looked away. She wasn't listening. He waited.

She spoke in a whisper, words meant for herself. "Everyone looked forward to your lectures. I lived in Chapel Hill that year. And every day I walked across campus on a carpet of petals from the dogwoods and the magnolias."

Simon sat back, flooded by the current of his own warm memories.

"It was a kind of fuzzy curtain that fell over Chapel Hill each spring. Thick air, heavy with perfume from the flowers. Do you remember?"

Simon felt uncomfortable with this. It wouldn't help either one of them if she couldn't see him as an authority figure. "You're making me homesick. But we're drifting. What about Mrs. Henning?"

"The point is, I was always cocky as a student. Sure of myself. I knew it all. That attitude was my bedrock. I had it then, and I've made use of it ever since." Martha stood, and walked toward the tall, narrow windows and looked out.

"You were bright, and a certain arrogance goes with that."

"So, the point is, when I saw Mrs. Henning, I was confident I could help her. Stupid, stupid me."

"An internist referred her," Simon prompted, "and you said something about, 'at the request of her husband'?"

"Wait a minute. I want to go back."

"All right."

Martha cast a cool green gaze at him. "First do no harm. Hippocrates' first proviso. The oath each physician takes. You taught it to us."

"Yes, because I believe in beginning with the basics. It's a simple precept, and, I think, an important one. There's a copy of it in my waiting room."

"That very first day in the lecture hall, you began by telling us that that oath was a sacred trust. It was a talk on ethics. You always had a strong aversion to playing God."

Simon shook his head. "We'd all love to be actors, and play God. That's why a lot of people become doctors. Tell me about Mrs. Henning."

Martha steeled herself, as if against some invisible foe, and took her time collecting her thoughts. "There was evidence of recent memory loss, and during the hour and a half she was in the office, I tried to pinpoint the cause. The results of the tests disturbed me."

"Ruined your hopes for an easy solution," Simon mused.

"Or a quick recovery."

"I should think, any recovery at all," he put in. "So, Mrs. Henning was in the early stages of Alzheimer's." Simon stroked his chin, remembering the first sting of being bested by that disease. "Rather young for an Alzheimer's patient."

"Yes, she was. But her mother had it, and her mother before her. So the history was there." Martha sat in the chair and leaned forward, green eyes blazing. "Simon, I had seen my share of debilitating illness. God, I'd treated psychotics and schizophrenics. And no matter how bad it was, there always seemed to be some medication—some pill they could take to at least offer some relief." Now her eyes glistened, and Simon filled the void.

"You seem, even now, overwrought by her condition. It's a road we've all been down. In fact, a psychiatrist with any degree of experience has seen these cases. Many of them. Even if it was your first, you're more upset than I'd have expected."

She nodded. "It's true. It's just that—" Martha paused and took a breath "—there's more to it."

"I see."

"The truth is, I've gotten myself into a situation that complicates the case."

"More complicated?" What could possibly make her case more difficult than it already was? So much for a quick resolution to this. He thought they'd spend a couple of afternoons talking, going over the facts. It'd be a simple, elementary affair, and then on to recover some of the lost years on a personal level.

"I haven't done anything to warrant this," she blurted out. "These charges—that I exercised poor judgment—they're ridiculous. I kept a close eye on Grace. I was on top of what she was doing, and how she felt, and the things that affected her. And I knew when she was happy..." Her voice caught, and he rose quickly, came around the desk, and bent over her, clasping her hands inside his own. They felt small and frail, or was that his imagination?

"Martha, listen. I know you're worried. I want you to know that I almost didn't take the case. I didn't think it was that serious. You could have had someone else." He looked down into the eyes he used to dream about.

"My career is at stake, Simon." Her voice was stronger now, and after an awkward pause, he rose, and sighed, and walked back around to his side of the room.

"Listen," he said, "I'll back you."

She looked up hopefully, and a silence stretched between them.

"Will you trust me?" he asked gently. She used to trust him. He gave her a chance to answer. When she didn't, he continued. "You have to let go of whatever it is. You can't harbor any hidden agenda. Do you want to be cleared?"

"I certainly hope to be cleared." Her voice faded.

"The charges say that you were negligent where Mrs. Henning was concerned. I'll only be able to help if I know—really understand—exactly what your impressions were at the time. You know," he added, "a decision can only be made at one moment in time. We can all look back and say there's been a bad decision. Only hindsight is twenty-twenty."

Martha nodded and let out a heavy sigh. She leaned back into the wingback and squinted, trying to recall.

"Grace was the perfect lady. I remember the first morning she came in so that I could get to know her. It was mid-morning and there she was in a silk dress, just dripping with diamonds. On anyone else they would have looked flashy, even lewd. But Grace Henning could carry it off like no one else I'd ever seen.

"She seemed glad to see me, and I asked how she was feeling. She said she felt fine. She sounded like an American. So different from Mr. Henning's clipped English accent. I wondered if she'd met her husband over here or abroad. It occurred to me to ask her if she was named for Grace Kelly, and she said, 'No. Grace Kelly?'

"Maybe she couldn't remember Grace Kelly. But she had that same style, the same shining smooth blond hair, perfectly styled. We walked down to what some of the residents called the Florida Room, and when we went in we had to strain to see against the strong rays of the sun...."

*

"We should have worn our sunglasses, Mrs. Henning."

The green of vines and the shiny curled leaves of plants took over the sunroom. White wicker furniture, plumped up with colorful flowered cotton cushions, dotted the perimeter, along with a few well-placed coffee tables.

"What beautiful material, Doctor Reed. Laura Ashley?" Grace eyed a comfortable loveseat.

"As a matter of fact, it is."

"What a beautiful place."

"I thought we could meet here, rather than in the office, the few times a week we have regular meetings. Right now, I have just a few questions."

But Grace was still off thinking about it being sunny. Martha checked herself, knowing her patient could often get stranded on one particular point.

"Yes, indeed, it is so sunny here," Grace said. "They say we're in for some bad weather. I hate bad weather. My flowers always die in the bad weather. But I see you have some lovely flowers here."

"We try to keep them healthy."

"I hope John is watching over the flowers at our house. Do you suppose he'll watch over the flowers, Doctor? Or should we write it in the orders?" She said it with a tiny smile, and the driest sense of humor.

Martha looked up, caught off guard, in time to see the merest glint in Grace's eye. "Yes, Grace. I'm sure he will. May I call you Grace?"

"Yes, please call me Grace."

"I need to do some diagnostic testing. Then, we'll be trying various medications until we decide the optimum course of your treatment." Martha reached into an envelope. "I'm going to show you three cards. And I want you to tell me what you see."

Grace leaned forward, folding her hands on the table, anxious to comply. Martha drew the cards.

"Yes. The cards are—I see three. There are three cards."

"And each of these cards has something different on it. The first is a number." Martha indicated and Grace nodded, watching.

"Um-hmm. I see."

"Now, the second is a picture of an object. And the third, is a line of objects, all the same size." Martha waited for Grace to get a good look at them.

"Now, I'm going to take the cards away, and I want you to tell me, if you can, what was on those three cards."

"Well, let me see. There was—I believe the first one was a letter. A number. Seven."

"Right. That's right."

Martha smiled, encouraged to see that her subject still had a good deal of her cognitive function.

"Take your time. The first one was the number seven."

"And the next—rain. It had to do with rain. Um, an umbrella."

"Yes. Good. Very good. And the third?"

Grace raised her head and spoke decisively. "A string of pearls."

"Fine," Martha said. "Very good. Now, I just have a few more questions, and our time will be up."

*

Martha stared across the desk at Simon. "It gave me an odd satisfaction that she'd err on the side of elegance."

Simon shook his head. "I don't follow."

"She was all elegance; and she was aptly named Grace. That third card was a picture of a row of marbles. If she had to get it wrong, it might as well have been a 'string of pearls'."

Chapter 2

SIMON TALBOT PULLED his jeep up to the front of his rough-hewn log house, tires grinding in a cloud of dust. He killed the engine, opened his door, and got out, then stopped. To listen. Whispering pines welcomed him to the peace and serenity of his home, nestled in the Adirondack preserve. The scent of pine filled his nostrils, and he closed his eyes, wanting to forget, still needing to remember. Subtracting the style from the substance would be his job, then sifting through it all. But his thoughts were interrupted by a throaty bark coming from the knotty pine structure. His devoted Lab beckoned, and he took the porch steps by twos to get to her, flinging the door open, bending down so Cindy could lick his face.

The golden Lab knew she was loved; that she performed some important function in the years since Simon had taken to the hills, seeking solace. Together they'd fished the streambeds looking for trout, and sat as the water told its stories. And it always seemed to make sense out here.

Simon ruffled the dog's furry ruff, then stepped inside to shower and change. Half an hour later he emerged from his bedroom, buttoning the smooth folds of a denim shirt. He stretched out on the comfortable sofa, and glanced around at the stone of the fireplace, and the reds and greens and browns of the woven rug at his feet. Too warm for a fire.

His dear friend Henry had actually tried to talk him into a gas fireplace. Gas! Here he was in the deepest, darkest land of pines. He drove dozens of extra miles to get here. He'd carved a rugged hideaway in an inhospitable mountain region, braved the snow and the ice and the frigid temperatures to live in this environment. And Henry wanted him to install a gas fireplace. Poor Henry. He really needed to be straightened out. Simon smiled at the thought of his dearest friend, and guessed that was what happened to successful men who wanted the aura, but not the inconvenience of rustic life.

He sighed and got up from his spot, heading for the door to find his loyal companion. Cindy bounded in, and sat looking up at him.

"What should we do now, girl?" She answered by curling up on the rug, looking back at her master, inviting him to join her. Simon gravitated toward the mantle and reached unconsciously for the photograph on the end, neatly framed in hardwood; silent, standing vigil. He took it down, staring closely at it.

There they were, sitting around the campfire: Martha, Joe Pritchard, Mike, Neil, and Jim Fenimore. All doctors, young and still impressionable. Martha was the only woman. And the brightest among them. He considered that, wondered if it had been a burden, then decided it hadn't. Courage through adversity. She'd had it then. Did she still? The day that picture was taken, he had escorted a group of medical students to a campsite for a survivalist weekend. The idea was conceived by a friend—another professor who was always coming up with wacky ideas to temper the boredom of the academic calendar.

Simon had been roped in to participating against his will. Two other senior members of the staff were committed to going, and it would have looked bad for him to back out. So, he tossed a sleeping bag and a knapsack full of gear into the back of the jeep, brought his beloved Cindy, and off they went. Cindy was a favorite with the students, which didn't surprise him. He loved her too.

Peering closer at the framed photo, he decided he looked better without the rugged beard he'd sported then. Five of his favorite students stared back at him. And he'd kept in touch with them. All but Martha. He traced his fingers absently over her image, then walked around to the alcove surrounded by bay windows and put the picture in the drawer of his desk. He sat, thinking. He thought about Martha and her patient, how the two women had bonded.

Cindy came over to lay near her master's feet. Fresh pine invaded his nostrils, and Cindy too had her nose in the air. The stillness was broken by two mourning doves, calling one to the other, married in a seamless rhythm of song.

"It's just the tip of the iceberg, girl," he said softly, scratching Cindy behind the ear. He stroked the dog's head, lost in thought. He was a master of his trade and the surest judge of human nature. Simon knew instinctively the papers only told him a small part of the story. What was it she'd started to tell him about it being more complicated? What on earth had she gotten herself into? The truth would surface and, when it did, he only hoped Martha would be on the winning side of it.

*

Simon rowed out into the middle of the lake. The water lapped up at the bottom of the wooden boat, and he pulled the oars back toward his lean chest with smooth, even strokes. He thought better out here on the water. Cindy had whined and pawed at his boots, even sat up to beg to be taken along, and he hated to leave her on the shore, tail wagging slightly, uncertainly. 'Why can't I come?' she had asked. And he couldn't give her a reason. He didn't know himself. Today it had to be just him, and the water, and the sounds of nature as a backdrop to his thoughts. There was too much to think about. A small voice told him that pining was for young men whose hearts were breaking for the first time. He was much too old for pining. Wasn't he? What were mature men allowed to do?

He intended to drop anchor just off one of a handful of tiny islands on Lake George. People camped here. Got a permit from the parks and recreation department and spent a lovely time communing with nature—boy scouts, senior citizens, lovers. Simon thought jealously of them, and it seemed suddenly there was nothing else in the world to think about. He pulled up his half-lowered anchor and pushed himself to row along the shoreline until his biceps burned and his back strained with the effort.

When *was it* Grace Henning had died—the tenth of November? And the investigation didn't begin to take shape until after December. More like January. All that time there had been paperwork shuffled back and forth between offices: Helsey, the health department, et cetera. He had been made aware of the investigation at about the end of March. That would be about right. It had been early spring. Unseasonably warm. They had called him in when it was determined that disciplinary action might be taken. How did these things roll downhill so fast? Martha happened to be in the way. Anybody would acquit her of any wrongdoing. Anybody. But he knew once they told him, he'd fight to be involved. Just in case.

It felt odd, even to him, that he should want to protect Martha after she'd let him down. Why couldn't he just let her go after what she'd done to him; after she had left him broken and emotionally vulnerable? He knew the answer was as simple as it was undeniable. He still loved her.

Simon turned the creaky wooden craft back in the direction of home, somehow satisfied he'd accomplished what he set out to do.

*

Martha returned to the neat confines of her apartment. A cursory look around told her that Jane had been by to clean. The lady came and went like a ghost, never obvious about her presence. Sometimes Martha was at home; sometimes she wasn't. But Jane would appear, bandana wrapped around her head, with her mops, pail, and plastic bag full of rags, all set to go. Jane never trusted anyone to have enough clean cotton rags, or the right thickness of rags to do the job, so she always brought her own. That was one of the first things she'd announced to Martha when she applied for the job. Jane had told her prospective employer that she knew her job, such as it was, and she didn't welcome anyone telling her what she needed or how to do it. Was that understood, she wanted to know? Yes, Martha told her. She understood. How long had she had Jane, she wondered absently as she hung her coat in the hall closet.

A few years, anyway. At least two? Martha was dependent on the woman to keep things tidy, even to take out the garbage on the right day. It was a symbiotic relationship; one of them needed the money; the other, the time.

She threw a frozen dinner into the microwave, reminding herself she'd have to stock up on those. She boiled water, made some herbal tea, then settled down to pour over the file she'd brought back from Simon's office. Today's meeting had daunted her. Not the facts of the case. God knew, she could recite them in her sleep. It was the whole setup. The climate of the hearing troubled her. What had begun as nothing more than an empty form that needed filling, had grown into an issue to be decided by an impartial tribunal. Impartial! Could Simon Talbot ever be truly impartial where she was concerned? It shocked her to think that the issue could take shape and gain momentum so quickly. If Simon wasn't part of it, somehow it would seem easier to stay on track, to concentrate. But intuition told Martha she had an ally in Simon, and she should be grateful for the way things had turned out.

The case folder absorbed her until she finished the last of her tea. She absentmindedly ate the scalding, tasteless meal, and went back for a refill of her drink. The light on her answering machine blinked incessantly. Martha considered checking it, but knew she wouldn't. She didn't want to be bothered. She clutched the file to her chest. Not now. She told herself this would be on her terms. There was a lot at stake. Her career was her life now, and no one would ever take that away! Simon would do a good job, despite the fact that at first she had felt otherwise. He'd be her champion. How insulted he must have been. She hadn't meant to be defensive. It seemed the frustration and lack of control were taking their toll.

Technically, she shouldn't be working. It was discretionary, and the board members had showed clemency in saying she'd be allowed to continue. It burned her up to think that after this ended, even if she was vindicated, these people who were ruining her life wouldn't so much as say they were sorry. Martha seethed at the thought of them: little bald men sitting in their ivory towers, not down in the trenches touching the patients with their hands, touching them with their lives.

Maybe she'd quit after they'd cleared her. It would serve them right. Let them try to find someone, anyone who would care deep down for patients the way she had. But she knew that only the patients would suffer if she chose to leave. The men in the towers would just look for another body.

Jane had left the laundry folded, the dishes washed, dried, and put away. Martha looked around approvingly. No countertop clutter, no sections of newspaper scattered on the coffee table, not even a used towel in the bathroom. *Perfect*, her mind told her. *Not perfect*, her heart intoned.

Who was she kidding? The apartment was orderly. It had no signs of life, and didn't look like a home to anyone. The rooms were devoid of any sense of love or being lived in. It was obvious she never spent any time here.

Where had the time gone? Martha stepped back into the kitchen, emptied the remainder of her tea into the sink, turned the cup upside down, and was seized with the urge to dirty a dish and leave it right there, in the middle of the sink. Instead she reached into an upper cabinet, pulling out a delicate stemmed glass with a deep-cut design. She opened the refrigerator, where she kept a bottle of chilled white wine for the occasional times when she wanted something to help her relax or to think.

Martha sipped the cool wine as she sauntered through the few tidy rooms that comprised the apartment. Beige. It struck her as odd that all the walls were some sort of tan color. Once in awhile it was set off with a cream, or a white, representing chance, not planning. The super had probably run out of his drab beige and substituted an old can of white. And, of course, she had never bothered about the colors of any of the rooms. Had she not even noticed? Not a priority. But how many weeks or months had slipped by, and it hadn't been important? The appliances in the kitchen were also some shade of white. They couldn't even match their ugly clashing color scheme. Who? The owners, the company, whoever it was who had bought out this complex four or five years ago. And yet it was not inexpensive to live here. The building was built with state-of-the-art conveniences; filled with upwardly mobile young people. *Just like you, Martha.*

And where are we all going?

If Grace Henning were still alive, she would have been appalled. There was a lady who had had real class. She'd had a sense of style that had stayed behind even after she herself left a room. That indefinable stamp of personality had been there in everything that her patient touched. Grace would have loved to give her decorating advice, she was sure.

It was like seeing the place for the very first time. Really, truly ugly, and quiet and dead. Martha was amazed at how uncomfortable she felt here, in what was supposed to be her own home. Life was passing her by while friends and family moved ahead with their lives. Yesterday's goals seemed unworthy of her life today. Medicine was what she'd expected it to be—exceeded all her expectations—but she never gave any thought to the years in the middle, when she'd be out on her own, and able at long last to afford expensive vacations and the nicer things in life. If only she'd considered whom she would share these years with.

The shrill ring of her cell phone startled her. She rushed to beat the third ring, then slid the button to *mute*.

Suppose it was him? *Stop calling me*, she willed. If only she could think. Put things into perspective; separate what had happened then, and what was happening now...

Maybe after Simon helped to clear her name, she could clear her head, and these phone calls would no longer be an issue.

Not ten minutes later, a knock at her door sent her scurrying to the peephole, glass in hand. Who would it be? She didn't want company. Not unexpected company. She considered it bad form to just show up on someone's doorstep. Her mother had subscribed to that belief from the beginning. So it was either a rude salesperson, or someone who had a right to show up unexpectedly. It could be a third possibility—someone trying to see her whom she didn't want to see.

A familiar voice called from the landing, "Martha? It's me."

Martha flung the door wide open.

"Susan!"

The younger Reed sister came bouncing into the room, auburn hair rolling over her shoulders and down her back.

"I tried to call. Where have you been?" Her sister looked impatiently at her watch, but Martha didn't mind. She broke into a smile, and gave the door an enthusiastic push, slamming it shut behind them.

"Come on in. You're just in time to join me in a glass of wine."

"Sounds great. I hope I'm not too far behind. Looks like you started without me." Susan glanced around, as though she suspected her sister was hiding someone. "You here alone?"

"Yep."

"How many glasses have you had?"

"Not enough."

The younger Reed flopped down on the couch, and focused in on her sister.

"Wine would be nice."

Martha walked around the small partition separating living room from kitchenette and got an extra glass.

"What are the folks doing tonight, Sue?"

"The usual."

"That sounds boring."

Susan glanced around the room. "Doesn't look too exciting here, either."

"True, so true." Martha laughed. "No dates tonight, Susie?"

"How come you, as the older sister, can ask me any personal questions, but if I asked you some of the same questions, you'd say I was impertinent?"

"True again." Martha took a seat and turned to look Susan squarely in the eye. "What do you want to know?"

"Everything. All about this trial or whatever it is. Mom and Dad stay up late every night talking about it."

"Do they?"

Susan would know. She'd been staying with them while Mom recuperated from hip surgery. Yes, she would know... It stabbed at Martha, the thought of her parents in their seventies, shouldering the pain and ambiguity of the last weeks. She wanted to shield them.

"They go over and over it," Susan said. "They want to help you. They talk about finding you a good lawyer."

"I don't need a lawyer. It's not that kind of hearing. The board members are brain dead, half of them. This is what happens in a system of any size whenever there's a fear of litigation."

"Who, though? I mean, how did it get started? Has somebody got it in for you, sis?"

"Nothing like that. It's just a matter of process. You know, like getting into an auto accident. Your insurance agency covers you, but they have to investigate. They have to fill out affidavits and get sworn statements. It has to be handled through channels. I've seen this before. It's not unusual. This is the first time I'm on the receiving end."

"I still don't like it."

"I don't either. I want it to be over just as much as Mom and Dad do." Martha lay back into the square pillow that matched the brown sofa. "What bothers me most—more than the inconvenience, and the humiliation—is that I liked this patient. She wasn't just another case to me. She was a special lady."

"That's what makes you a remarkable doctor. The sympathy you have for people. It's not easy to come by these days. Promise me one thing."

"What?" Martha took a small sip of wine.

"Whatever the outcome, you won't cut us off—Mom and Dad and me. I want you to know we're here." Susan's eyes welled, and she quickly looked away.

Martha leaned over and put arms around her sister. "Just remember, I haven't done anything wrong."

Chapter 3

TWO DAYS LATER, Simon leaned back in his office chair. Its groan echoed how he felt about these proceedings. Tedious. No other word to describe it.

"Just pick up with what happened next, will you?" he told Martha. "Refer to your notes if you have them. This isn't testimony, and it isn't an examination before trial. So you can go back and change your mind if it isn't right. Again, nothing is written in stone."

"On the twentieth of January, John Henning came to see me at my office at Helsey," Martha said. "He was a refined, intelligent man of about fifty-five, distinctly British. Mr. Henning is an attorney here in Albany. When I met him, my first impression was that he was attractive and well-spoken. Aristocratic, almost."

Simon said nothing, but leaned back in the groaning chair, holding a fountain pen, pensive. Refusing to make eye contact.

Martha had the story in her head and clearly wanted to tell it without being interrupted. She leaned back herself and took a long, deep breath. The cadence of her speech changed perceptibly. The story obviously came easily to her as the bits and pieces of the meeting crystallized.

"We were at my office at Helsey. John Henning asked me if his wife was going to get any better. I told him no, and that I wished it wasn't the case. In fact, I said, 'She'll most likely grow steadily worse.'

"He was upset. He asked me how? Why? Was this as a result of something she'd done or taken? And I said, 'No, that it isn't like cigarette smoking, where you can pinpoint a reason for the illness; a cause and effect. The research was in its early stages.'

"It was the hardest thing I'd ever had to explain to the spouse of a patient. He'd be her caretaker and I wondered if he realized it…"

*

"It sneaks up sometimes, Mr. Henning," Martha told Grace's husband. "Can you give me any information as to how she's been lately? For example, when exactly did she start exhibiting symptoms of memory loss and personality change?"

"Well, it's been several months since I began to suspect something wasn't quite right."

Martha sat upright.

"Several months? Why, may I ask, did you wait so long?"

"To have it checked out?"

"Yes."

Henning took umbrage. "You have to understand, Dr. Reed, that at first I wasn't sure. I felt I must be overreacting; that it wasn't serious enough to warrant doing anything. She had trouble sleeping. I'd catch her up walking around in the middle of the night."

"Anything else?"

"Well, I noticed that she wasn't as together as she usually was. And she'd never had those problems before."

"Can you be more specific?"

"Grace was never one to be caught with a run in her stocking, or wearing an outfit without a matching pair of shoes. She was always well put together. It was little things, here and there, that gave clues. And then, of course, there was the cocktail party."

Mr. Henning crossed one leg over the other, and Martha caught the heavy scent of fresh leather and noticed his exquisite shoes. The kind of shoes one brings home from a trip to Italy. Custom-made. She considered him, and Grace, and knew inherently that it was all somehow important.

"It was the cocktail party that made it all clear to me. I just couldn't ignore it any longer." He shook his head. "It was a disaster."

"Whose party?"

"Ours. An annual event. The Winterfest, we called it, and it took place in December here in Saratoga just before we travelled to New Orleans to spend the winter with Jack and Vera."

"Can you relate the details to me?"

"We were standing in the dining room, around the punch bowl. We'd made it a black tie affair. Everyone was dressed to the nines. Grace looked beautiful, as always. She came floating down the staircase to a gathering of about a dozen friends—close friends. They were the same group that belonged to our country club; the same we'd cruised with, and rented beach houses next to. The Winterfest was a sort of prelude to the holiday season. Grace and I stood by the door, greeting people as they arrived."

"Was there much confusion?"

"There wasn't, really. Just a fair amount of gaiety, as you might expect. But nothing resembling confusion, no."

"You were very social?"

"We took parties and entertaining in stride, yes."

"So—"

"So the guests dribbled in a few at a time, and Grace offered punch in the dining room while I took coats. We served a traditional English Yuletide drink from a recipe that had been in Grace's family going back for a century."

"Grace's family."

"Yes. They're an old European family. She's more English than I am." He smiled. "It was a heavy, fragrant brew, with a dark, almost ruby, color, and it was spiked with quite a bit of alcohol." Martha listened and thought about how engaging Grace's husband was. A charming man, who could make even a gruesome story compelling.

"Now, there was one new couple who came: the Gladleys. And they'd never had our punch before. At some point Louise Gladley approached Grace and asked her for a cup. Grace poured it and then handed it to her. Louise tasted the drink. She loved it. She asked Grace what it was. Suddenly, Grace was at a loss. Not only couldn't she remember the punch, it was obvious that she didn't know who Louise was, either. Grace scowled at Louise, really *scowled*, and told her to 'just *drink* it.' It was the most embarrassing thing you could imagine.

"The room stood still. Everything just stopped, and no one really knew how to recover. Vera Whitworth was there, from New Orleans. She and Jack are probably our oldest friends, since Grace and Vera first met at finishing school. Vera caught on and rallied to mediate the situation, but Grace was flustered. She excused herself, and went running up to her room. I tried to step in. I made excuses and said she hadn't been feeling well. But, really, it was so out of character for Grace, they all knew that something was terribly wrong." Henning looked away, squinting and shaking his head.

"None of them could quite bring themselves to step out of the correct places they felt comfortable in, and it seems we were all a room full of strangers. I just wanted to get upstairs to my wife and figure out what was wrong with her, and how this could happen without any warning."

"Mr. Henning, the point is that there probably were warning signs, but you weren't expecting them, and you weren't equipped to recognize them, so it isn't surprising that it took something so blatant for you to see it."

"What can I expect, Dr. Reed?"

Martha was hard pressed to come up with something positive.

"Well, as time goes on, most patients lose their ability to think abstractly and to carry on many of their daily functions. And there are personality changes, which, of course, you've already noticed. Sometimes, there's a loss of inhibition, or the concept of time. Some suffer from aggression; others, withdrawal. The motor skills weaken. The list goes on and on."

"I see. I want you to give me the bad news all at once. Please don't try to spare me. Where does this illness come from, and how is it cured?"

"I'm afraid there isn't a cure at this time. In many ways, it's an enigma."

Henning shifted in his seat, looking annoyed. "Don't patronize me, Dr. Reed."

"Some patients can't remember people, or events. Or even words for common things. That sounds like what's been happening to your wife. Mrs. Henning's dementia might include delusions—misinterpretations of real events. Or hallucinations, which are themselves unreal events."

Henning rubbed his chin thoughtfully. "Are you sure about all of these symptoms?"

"I'm afraid so. But there are ways of coping with, or at least getting around some of the problems."

Henning stood and paced the office as she explained. He seemed distracted to the point that she wasn't certain he heard that she said the disease was degenerative. She soldiered on with the dubious honor of explaining to him that he could no longer expect to continue his married life as he knew it, and that his wife's condition would only worsen.

"You might consider placing Grace at the Helsey Institute while her medication is adjusted and she has further evaluation."

"Will you continue to treat her?"

"You're free to choose any physician you like, but certainly I'd be happy to work with Grace, if that's what you want."

"Can she travel? I want to take her to New Orleans."

"Y-es," Martha said slowly, "but have her come in to see me before you plan any trips, and then you can have her check in when you return for more assessments. I'll begin treating her with a daily dose of Aricept."

John Henning shifted, turning from the sunlight at the window. Martha felt guilty, and watched as he buried his face in his hands.

"Mr. Henning, would you like some time alone?"

"No. Thank you." The man looked weary.

"Do you think I should keep her at home?"

Martha sensed his distress. "Would keeping her at home present problems?"

Another pause, as he considered her question.

"One would have to define 'problems,' Dr. Reed. Do I think keeping Grace at home would be wise? Advisable? Whose agenda are we serving?"

The question hung in midair.

Martha floundered. "Well, certainly, Grace's well being; her welfare is all that matters. Patients thrive on familiar, well-known settings, such as home."

"You'd like me to keep her at home. Hire a few health care workers while I'm away. You know, I'm out of town quite a bit." He paused as if debating whether to go on. "Let me ask you, have you ever encountered the reality of today's auxiliary health care workers? Have you?"

Martha shifted in her seat. What was he getting at?

"The truth is, Dr. Reed, that one is better off having a loved one committed to a trusted facility than to take one's chances with an aide. To be perfectly honest, I don't feel comfortable taking chances with a home health aide for my wife. There isn't the system of checks and balances as with an institution. Helsey gives me a feeling of hope. Some feeling of peace, knowing I'm dealing with the best institution possible. And yet I'm asking you if I can take her to New Orleans. I know this sounds like a contradiction. The truth is that I couldn't live with myself if I didn't give my wife this one last chance to enjoy our New Orleans visit. It's just a tradition… Can you understand that, Dr. Reed?"

*

The room was quiet, save for the ticking clock, and the furious scratching of Simon Talbot's fountain pen.

"Aricept, once a day?" Simon spoke as he wrote.

"Yes."

"Anything else?"

"Yes. John smiled a slow, sad smile, which I'll always remember. He stood and thanked me. Then he turned and left the office. He'd agreed to bring her in as soon as he could."

Simon shifted, cast Martha a sidelong glance. "'John,' is it now?"

"I've told you, Simon. There is much more to it than the records indicate."

"All right. You were on the noble path, to save this woman from an incurable disease."

"Very funny, Simon." She cast him a sour look. He was irritated, and Martha made a mental note to go slowly. Ease him into it so that he understood the circumstances. If she didn't set it up right, Simon would be a formidable factor to deal with.

"Continue." He was already back to his notes.

"In 1891, Sigmund Freud published his treatise on neurological brain disorder—where the ability to pronounce words is lost because of organic brain disease."

"*On Aphasia.*" Simon smiled, as if pleased at his own handiwork as a teacher.

"And looking back, it was at about that time in Grace's treatment that I began to read Freud's *The Interpretation of Dreams.*"

"Do dreams figure heavily in the case?"

She looked away and muttered, "Only my own."

Chapter 4

"GRACE WALTZED IN, smiling. I remember she had a suit on that day. It was a crisp, off-white, almost a cream color. And she told me it was Chanel." Martha laughed. "I know I sound totally affected by…"

"Were you affected by it?" Simon's eyes narrowed.

"What?"

"You know…" He frowned. "By the affluence, and the power. Or the money. Money usually means power. At least to some people."

"No. Of course not. It was only a matter of seeing her as a woman first."

"And a patient second?" he prompted.

"Not second in that her status as my patient was second to my impressions of her clothes. But in that she was a woman first, Simon. You have to understand that I identified with her as a mature, sophisticated woman. I'd like to think of myself as somewhat in that league."

"You are." Simon looked past her, his face unreadable. Was he thinking of her then, or only now? She watched as he brought himself back with effort and refocused.

"How did you find her at that point?" he asked.

"I'd say when she first came in, she was near normal, or what I'd expect her to be. There really weren't any deficit signs. She was quite clear on things, and I couldn't see any indications that her long-term memory had been altered."

"What was the specific purpose of this particular meeting? You'd already given the go-ahead for her husband to take her south, hadn't you?"

"I wanted to see her again. I didn't know her well enough. It occurred to me that I'd have to move quickly to establish a baseline profile of Grace's personality in order to have something to compare it with later on."

"You wanted more of a personal assessment, then."

"Wouldn't you?"

"Absolutely. Oh, I agree with everything I've heard so far, Martha. You'll never have to convince me. Only the others. The powers that be." And then he added, "If it were up to me, we'd be sitting over a few cocktails, talking over old times, not embroiled in this mess. But that isn't my place. Not now."

Martha gave him a caustic look. "Do us both a favor, Simon, don't make this into a personal issue between you and me. I have no interest in what may or may not be happening under different circumstances. We're here to talk about Grace."

"You're absolutely right." He nodded. "I stand corrected."

She'd made the point, and he'd conceded, though somehow Martha felt she'd lost the battle. You couldn't shame or embarrass the likes of Simon Talbot. Somehow the bastard always came out smelling like a rose.

"I did manage to get an in-depth picture of where she was coming from. And it helped. She spoke to me about her life, and their friends, and about Mr. Henning as well."

Martha flipped open the spiral notebook and read from it, reliving the day when Grace had come into the office, happy and smiling…

*

"I know you're planning a trip to New Orleans. Mr. Henning said he'd like you to see the Whitworths."

"We haven't seen them since the holiday party."Grace caught herself.

"It's all right. You're bound to forget things."

The happiness vanished and Grace shook her head annoyed. "You see, Doctor Reed. You say I have this Alzheimer's disease, and perhaps I do. But everything I forget, every little thing, will be blamed on that disease. I won't even be allowed to forget the simplest things."

"I understand your concern. And I will try to separate which symptoms are attributed to the disease from those that aren't. That's a good point, and I can assure you I'm aware of it."

"Even things that anyone would say in ordinary conversation will be twisted around to prove what people think about my having this disease."

"No, no. I promise you I'm going to be paying very close attention."

Grace sat back, relieved. She took the glass of water Martha offered her, sipped it, then put it down, chin up, ready to go on.

"I'd like to start by having you tell me about your normal life; the way that you and Mr. Henning spent time."

"Well, we've lived our lives in cycles."

"What do you mean?"

"We're like the snowbirds from year to year, traveling during the same times. Summers in the North, winters down South. I suppose we've been just a little bit spoiled all these years."

"In what way?"

"I am distantly related to an old European family, or so I'm told. My father died when I was young. I don't remember him, but he and my mother didn't get along from what I could gather. She was a cold woman."

"Did she treat you coldly?"

"From the look of things, she gave us everything: plenty of toys, vacations, and camps where we'd be gone all summer. I grew up on a nanny's lap, away at private schools where I wore the 'best' clothes, and made the 'best' friends. All I ever really wanted was to have a little piece of her to myself. But that was the one thing she'd never give."

"You sound bitter."

"I'm not, really, just disappointed. Life is such a disappointment, don't you think, Dr. Reed? Don't you think that life is a disappointment?"

"I suppose it is. Sometimes we just make the best of it. Now, you said 'we.' Do you have siblings?"

"A brother, Joel. He was a sweet little boy. He died when he was ten. Joel was with us just long enough to leave a terrible void when he passed on."

"I'm sorry."

"It was many years ago, and I've put it behind me now and made my investment in tears. John always says a good investment is worth all the world, but a bad one is a terrible waste. It never pays off. You have to cut your losses and go on."

"Sounds like you're heavily into the stock market," Martha commented.

"We've had our share of investments."

Grace looked off, preoccupied. "Saratoga was brimming with life in August. Every year for a hundred years people had flocked in, to gamble at the tables, and to settle in to the grand hotels on Broadway and the private homes on Union Avenue. Some of them moved in to summer residences that had been left vacant. Most of the people who came there, for the track or polo, spent winters on the continent. They saw the season as a tradition they couldn't do without."

"Did you and your husband spend a lot of time there?"

"We own a house in town. Quite a lovely house, really, with Victorian gingerbread trim, and a wonderful wrap-around porch. We fill it with colorful furniture, and baskets of geraniums all around."

Grace had obviously tapped into a mainline, and Martha struggled to keep a mental diary of all she'd been told, still conveying her interest, knowing that to interject would be a mistake.

"We spent lots of time there, long after the crowds had left the racetrack and the red-and-white awnings had come down. We used to walk down the avenue to Yaddo, the artists' retreat. And we enjoyed watching the change of seasons there. The house was lavish, even by my standards. It was a stone's throw from the Oklahoma Track. Twenty years ago, some friends had talked us into buying a thoroughbred, and we raced him. Just there at Saratoga, you see. Nowhere else. Simply for the pleasure of it and the thrill of seeing our horse coming down the homestretch. There's a thunder in the air when they gallop by. Have you ever heard it? Do you know what I mean?"

Martha nodded, afraid to break the spell.

"And there was the Whitney Gala. You know, the one Mary Lou puts on every year. It's another Saratoga tradition. We'd see all our old friends that came up from New York then."

Grace went on to describe film stars, bankers, and socialites; another world that Grace had grown up in, but that Martha had only read about.

"What did you and your husband do during the winter?" Martha asked.

"Sometimes we stayed in Saratoga. It's a lovely, quiet place when the snow covers everything. You can wrap yourself in fur and walk along the street under the street lamps, and go into the shops. And then, there was Christmas…"

Grace trailed off, and Martha wondered if she was thinking about this last Christmas, and if she knew that it would be, forever and always, the turning point from which there was no going back. Grace rallied after a moment, and said they spent January and February in Palm Beach. They'd close up the house on Union Avenue and move down. John felt it was better to close up in the off season than to stay, and she said he encouraged her to cut short the longer season in the Northeast. It seemed there was a whole contingent going south.

*

Simon and Martha made eye contact. Then she closed the spiral notepad, and he went back to his writing.

"Grace said she always resisted, until the last moment." Martha leaned back, depleted. "The session lasted a full hour that day. I had just concluded that Grace was as cognizant as you or I."

Simon's fountain pen froze. "What made you change your mind?"

"When she went to leave. She picked up the letter opener I had sitting on my desk. She'd been eyeing it for some time, and I thought she was admiring the design. But she handed it to me, and said, 'I think you should throw this away.' I said, 'Throw it away?' And she said, 'Why, you certainly can't write with it.'

"It annoyed me to see her do those little things that gave away her illness, despite the fact that she was only doing what Alzheimer's patients do.

"I gave my report to Mr. Henning. He came in to the office the next day. He was British, did I mention that?"

Simon nodded, looking grim.

"I discovered that the first time he opened his mouth. The words slipped out like quicksilver." Martha lost focus, then bit her lower lip and pulled herself back with effort. "I found out he was a prominent attorney who ran a successful practice. He looked the part: polished, polite, and precise. I invited him to sit down, and told him about my observations so far. I said a change of scenery was okay…so long as he recognized, from then on, what was important was giving her a routine and not the change of pace. It was the routine that she'd have to hold on to. Predictable events, well-known surroundings. I stressed this would make her feel secure. The ordinary and the familiar, to keep her grasp of things. I knew Mr. Henning had reluctantly decided to have Grace committed. It was my job to convince him that she'd be comfortable at the sanitarium. I told him not to worry, that Grace would be happy at Helsey. I told him that she would probably outlive us all.

"He seemed to take it pretty well. We made plans to get things moving: start the paperwork, prepare Grace mentally for the move, and get her in residence soon.

"Mr. Henning saw me a few days later. I thought he had some question about her insurance status, but instead he wanted to talk about taking his wife on the trip that they'd planned.

"I voiced concern about him taking Grace down to New Orleans because it took her entirely out of the loop. I'd have no influence over her there—no contact with either of them. He just kept telling me that it would disappoint his wife, and it made me feel guilty somehow, that she wouldn't have this one last visit.

"There would be a lot of changes—lifestyle changes—and Grace would be unaware of many of them; it would become almost a custodial situation.

"When he got up to leave, he shook my hand, and held it just a moment longer than necessary. I thought he looked into my face, reading me—asking himself, maybe, if we were making the right choices. I wished him a good trip."

Martha sighed and shook her head, avoiding Simon's penetrating look. "I admired and respected him for his strength and his dignity in the face of it all. I couldn't imagine what he must be going through, and I invited him to contact me with any further questions. I fought back the impulse to apologize that I couldn't do more."

Martha waited. Whatever Simon thought, he was keeping it to himself.

"Mr. Henning went home then, and they prepared for their trip," she said. "At that point I had no idea how rapidly the disease would progress, and my patient would decline."

Simon shifted, unsettled, and focused on a sinking ship on the wall behind Martha. With each passing minute, the doomed vessel had more meaning.

"So," he said, "it was a simple case of damage control, as it is with Alzheimer's. No possibility of a cure. Only adjustment. Action and reaction as things progressed."

"That's what I thought," Martha mused. "A typical case."

*

At two a.m. Simon tossed the bedcovers aside, sat up, and clicked on the lamp. He rolled out of bed and grabbed his robe. For him there would be no sleep.

Nancy Ryan, his secretary, had photocopied every scrap of paper relating to Martha's case since the beginning. Maybe even before that. Nancy had the intuitive sense that some of the best secretaries had, knowing what their employers wanted even before they knew themselves. Simon pondered Nancy, the twenty-seven-year-old woman who'd worked in the outer office for the past three years, answering his calls, taking his messages, fending off drug reps from the pharmaceutical companies. They came at her with offers of concert tickets and dinners, even vacations to be spent learning about the new drugs, and the latest research. As the gatekeeper, Nancy had to deflect them. Make excuses and not leave any bruises. She did this with aplomb. Nancy was fearless in shark-filled waters.

But with him it was a vastly different story. She crept in to leave papers on his desk. She was respectful, almost reverent. When she called him at home, the few times she did, she referred to him as "Dr. Talbot" despite the fact that he'd told her repeatedly to call him by his first name, especially when they were outside the office. "It's all right at work," he told her. "It's just a title, and it has its place. But you don't have to call me 'doctor' when we're not on duty." She never listened. Cute, sweet Nancy.

Simon handled the batch of papers she sent with the file. He smiled, looking down absently. The smile died on his lips when he read the name on it: Henning/Reed.

Anyone else's case and he could have kept it contained in its folder, neatly tucked away in a drawer. Not this one.

He considered for a moment the irony of his position, to access someone else's judgment. Had Martha been responsible for the accident? Not directly responsible, no. Of course not. But indirectly, unwittingly responsible? That bothered him. He asked himself how he'd be impartial when he was so involved emotionally. Yes, there was no denying it. It might have been yesterday that they had fallen out. Time had no meaning in a self-imposed oblivion. In five years, all he'd done was work and study, write papers, give lectures, and immerse himself in the lives of his patients. He tried to help them, and lived vicariously through them sometimes, but it hadn't been enough to wipe Martha out of his mind. He knew that now.

The cabin served as an oasis. When it was built, he'd intended to use it as a weekend home. It was just far enough from his office to give him pause in the dead of winter. A peaceful summer drive, it could be a nightmare in the winter, when ice clung to the underpasses of bridges and cars collided on the slick surface of the road. Despite the fact that he'd bought four-wheel-drive vehicles, there was still a nagging insecurity accompanying him down the mountain, his mind racing with contingency plans.

One of his neighbors had said there was a sublime integrity to being able to tough it out up here in the winter season. Certainly, it taught one to survive. Physically survive. Mentally, it was a lonely place in the cold. During those months—and they were long—there was only the sizzling fire, and good books, and Cindy.

A cup of hot coffee, and a freshly blazing fire, and Cindy. Pleasant companions, such as they were. Tonight they seemed inadequate to him. Somehow this lovely picture of nature at its finest was incomplete. He stroked Cindy's head absently. He loved her, as much as a man could ever love a dog. And somewhere inside he came face to face with the fact that he needed another kind of love. Had needed it all along.

He'd read the transcript of their meeting, even if it took all night. And then be ready when she came to the office, and told him more of the story. He'd listen with uncompromising ears, and then he'd ask her some questions of his own.

Chapter 5

AT TEN A.M., Martha Reed pulled into the parking lot of the medical arts building. Simon watched from his window as she carried her purse and a paper bag into the building. Yesterday's severe attire had been abandoned, and today she wore a pea-green jacket with matching slacks, and a beige silk tee underneath. A simple gold chain adorned her neck, and her pumps were low, almost flat shoes. Simon grinned when he saw her. From outward appearances, she was more comfortable today.

"Here, Simon, I brought the sweets." She dropped smoothly into a chair.

"Well now, Martha, you look like you're headed for lunch with an old friend." *I could have been that old friend*, he brooded.

"Am I too casual?"

"Not at all. I'm glad you've toned it down a little. It means you've decided to relax, about the hearing, and everything else."

"But I could be just pretending to be casual, to throw you off. Suppose I'd been guilty of flagrant misconduct? I could be pretending not to take it seriously, to cloud the issue."

"Yes, Martha, you could be doing any one of a number of things. What kinds of donuts did you bring?"

"Oh, everything I remembered you liked: cinnamon and cider donuts, those French crullers…"

She remembered his taste in donuts. This touched him, and he sat watching her, and smiled absently until she did a double take and wanted to know if he was all right.

"Fine." He was still smiling. "What do you say we go on with the story?"

Martha made a cursory pass through her notes and shook her head. "I need to try to make sense of these."

Simon folded his hands. He was tired. "You were telling me that Mr. Henning had wanted to take his wife out of town. That, in fact, they left for New Orleans."

"Somewhere I wrote down…here it is." She scanned the notebook. "I have a summary of that visit when she returned. Do you want me to read it?"

"Please."

She cleared her throat.

"Grace looked refreshed when she came back. It was obvious, even in the way she carried herself. I told her she was looking well, and that the trip to New Orleans must have done her some good. She brightened when I said that. It made her happy. I asked her about it…"

∗

"Let's talk about the trip to New Orleans, shall we?"

"It was cold in Saratoga. You know what it's like, Doctor."

"Yes, I'm afraid I do. Go on."

"We went to visit Vera and Jack."

"The Whitworths."

∗

"She stopped, as if the connecting parts of the story eluded her. At first I let it go. I didn't want to disturb her train of thought. But as the moments dragged on, I was afraid that she might never retrieve some integral part of her story, and I was disturbed by that; so finally, I did prod her."

∗

"You mentioned the Whitworths. Old friends, you've said. And, I take it they lived near the city of New Orleans?"

Grace stared blankly. "New Orleans. Yes, we went to see Vera. It was Mardi Gras. The house is grand, you know. In the old style. You know the thing?"

"Mm-hmm." Martha made a notation: *Uses 'thing' to replace forgotten words and phrases*. She scribbled it quickly, still trying to keep the thread of Grace's story.

"Old style…" Grace was squinting at something invisible. "White hard thing—brick."

"White-painted brick? I've seen that a lot in the South. Did the Whitworths have a porch? That's another thing that's common there. It's almost a stereotype, the large wooden porch with rocking chairs. Lemonade on the porch and—"

"Lemonade!" Grace seized on the word. "We had lemonade."

Martha tried to bring her back, knowing that digression would be the rule, and Grace went on to say that they flew to the airport, then rented a car for the drive to the Whitworths. From what she told Martha, the Hennings were a traditional couple who repeated many of the same customs from year to year. And apparently one of those was for Jack and Vera, and John and Grace, to get together in February for Mardi Gras.

"You'd known the Whitworths for many years, I take it?"

"They were peach farmers seventy-five years ago. Maybe more."

"Oh?"

"In Georgia. They moved to Louisiana and ran a cotton mill. So they were in…dustrious. They were industrious."

"It certainly sounds like it."

"They had plenty of money," Grace confirmed. She went on to say that she and Vera had met at private school in New York. Vera had been sent way up North, and she was feeling homesick and ill at ease. Grace befriended her. The two had been inseparable from then on.

"We drove past the stone wall that went around the house," Grace said. "The wall ended at a drive with a heavy, wrought iron gate. It was a grand old house, did I say that? A Southern home, you know. With a garden filled with colorful flowers, and old trees."

Martha listened to the vivid picture painted by her patient. She made a note that Grace had been excited about being there. Nothing, Grace said, ever seemed to change at the Whitworths; when you drove onto the property, it was like going back in time.

"But John was cautious. He made me promise I wouldn't overdo. I wasn't to tire myself out with a whirlwind of parties. We always had such late parties down there. We went to the clubs and had card games."

"It sounds wonderful. Can you tell me about the city?"

"It's a fine city. Shipping is important there, and tourism. The French Quarter has houses all painted with bright colors, on narrow streets. They have painted shutters on either side of the doors, and the windows, of course. And you can see the French and Spanish influence there. In Jackson Square…that's where the artists sit, and, as a matter of fact, I had an uncle who painted portraits at Jackson Square. His name was Ray. Mother cringed when Uncle

Ray told stories about the things that went on down there. Especially during the Mardi Gras season."

Grace took a hiatus from the story, and melted in her chair with a little, wistful smile. She must have been traveling back, remembering her uncle. Martha marveled at the clarity of her memory, and the flavor in the way she related the details. She made a note that Grace's long-term memory was well intact, and that Grace had an excellent grasp of detail.

"Go on."

"And all over there are fine old nineteenth-century homes. French explorers staked out the land in the early seventeen-hundreds. But I think one of the most interesting things about the city is the influence of voodoo. Marie Laveau was the queen of voodoo, and she was an important figure in the city."

"Fascinating!"

"Jazz began there, you know. Some say Kansas City, but I say it was in New Orleans. And when we went down, over the years, John and Jack had to walk down Royal Street at least once. Late in the day, or early in the evening, the two of them were always poking their heads into the shops and buying art or looking at antiques. Jack and Vera lived just outside the Garden District. Their house was built in eighteen-hundred-something…eighteen-fifty, maybe. And one day, we all went to the Café du Monde to hear the jazz."

For a time, Grace was clearly back in New Orleans—just as she had been years before, with her closest friends. She described how the strains of jazz drifted up the streets and down the alleys. The Whitworths hadn't changed. They were a little gray around the edges. They were all slowing down. Just four very dear friends, who could be parted for years, meet again, and never skip a beat. Grace said they spent most of the afternoon catching up at the café, and then decided to return home. There were cocktail parties—Grace would later describe them in great detail. And she seemed to remember every aspect, in spite of her condition.

*

It was Fat Tuesday. A night to celebrate and indulge before Lent. And all of the city was thrown into the rhythm and mood of the Mardi Gras. The Hennings had spent a quiet day. Vera and Jack took them on a tour of one of the cotton plantations, then they'd all come back for lunch. Mabel Smith, a cheerful, robust woman, served lunch on the sun porch in back of the house. It was a screened-in section to keep out the insects.

Mabel was the housemaid, and she had been working at the Whitworth house for about twenty years. She was almost furniture. Mabel went about her duties, and was scheduled to leave around six. The maid rounded a corner and bumped into her, poised at the top of the staircase, listening to John and Vera. Grace hadn't planned to listen, but happened to be in the right place at the right time.

"It's just a bad idea for her to be in those crowds," John's voice floated up.

"You want her to miss the parade? At Mardi Gras!"

Mabel's eyes went wide and she rolled them. "They'ze talkin' 'bout you, Miss," she whispered.

"Yes. Do you mind if I listen?" Grace asked politely.

"Do y'all mind if I do?"

With that, Grace squeezed behind the rotund black woman and flattened herself against the wall. Their shadows fell grotesquely along the plaster while they strained to hear.

"That's probably the last place in the world for her to be in view of her condition. Vera, the doctor says she needs peaceful surroundings."

"Well, I suppose the noise of the parade and the unruly crowds would be a dreadful thing to expose her to. It just seems…Mardi Gras without Grace. It isn't going to be the same."

"Nothing is the same anymore." He said it with resignation, and Grace moved from behind Mabel and dropped to sit at the top of the landing, clinging to the banister, saddened by the forsaken tone of her husband's voice.

"Well, my house is familiar, even though it's been a few years. Shame on you, John! She'll be fine. Mabel is just finishing up. I'll have her make lemonade. She makes the best you've ever tasted, with mint from the garden. She'll bring some out and serve it on the porch. Before you know it, we'll be back."

He must have been unsure, because nothing was said until Vera finally spoke again.

"If you'd rather, we can stay home. We don't have to go to the parade. Lord knows, Jack and I have seen plenty of them. Sometimes we go away just to escape the madness."

"No, it's all right. We'll go. Of course, we'll go."

Mabel started down the stairs as if on cue. Grace stood and followed her.

John appeared at the bottom and looked up at his wife. When she reached the foyer, he put an arm around her. "How are you feeling, darling?"

"Oh, I'm fine. I thought I'd pass on the parade, though."

"Really?" He seemed surprised.

"Yes, it's been a long day, and I think I'll just sit and read my novel."

"Very well, then." John put his arms around Grace and nuzzled her with a kiss. "That's fine, darling. I'll set your novel in the front parlor by the easy chair. Please put your feet up and take it easy. Rest." John kissed Grace on both cheeks, and Vera called up to her husband, "Jack! Ash Wednesday is coming."

Mabel came from the coat closet; a model of deportment in a gray dress, white collar, and apron, carrying a shawl. She opened the lacy material and put it gently around Vera's shoulders. Grace noticed she didn't look up and felt she was secretly amused.

"Thank you," Vera nodded. "Oh, Mabel, would you be so kind as to make some of that fabulous lemonade of yours? The one with the sprigs of mint. And serve it to Mrs. Henning on the front porch?"

"Yes, ma'am."

"Just take the tray out onto the veranda, and maybe add a few lemon cookies or cucumber sandwiches. Do that last thing before you leave, please."

"Yes, ma'am, I will."

"Make sure the lemons are fresh squeezed, Mabel. Thank you."

Grace and Mabel exchanged a secret smile over Vera's head. Mabel had been making her lemonade for the last twenty years, yet Vera never hesitated to give her instructions about how to put together the recipe.

Jack came down finally; they all said their good-byes and the three left.

With the others gone, Grace was free to spend her time as she chose. She went out onto the porch, and walked around the side of the house, looking at the garden. Mabel came out carrying a large silver tray covered with white linen. Grace felt that it was a lot of fuss for a glass of lemonade. But she wasn't terribly surprised. It was like that in the South. The screen door slammed behind Mabel.

"Here we is, ma'am. The best drink in Dixieland."

"Thank you, Mabel. You really didn't have to go to this trouble."

"They'ze my orders, ma'am. Miz Whitworth runs a tight ship."

Mabel watched Grace eye the glass for a moment, and said, "Miz Henning, would you be wantin' somethin' more powaful?"

"I beg your pardon?"

"Maybe you want a mint julep. We could keep the mint, and put in a little Jack Daniels."

"Why, Mabel!"

"I'm sorry, ma'am. I didn't mean no disrespect. I was just tryin' to make you feel comfortable, you understand... I didn't mean..."

"I think that's a wonderful idea. Do you know how long it's been since I've had a real mint julep?"

"How long, Miz Henning?"

At first she said nothing; then Grace laughed. "Well, right now I can't remember. My condition, you know. But odds are it's been a pretty long time."

Mabel started for the screen door. "You just leave everything to me, ma'am. You mighta missed the Mardi

Gras parade, but after you have one'a my mint juleps, it'll seem like the real party is right here. You'll be feelin' sorry for those poor people that had to stand in the streets."

She left, and Grace chuckled. What a charming companion Mabel had turned out to be. Mabel entered the house, and Grace walked the length of the porch, eyeing the flowers. The garden was brimming with blossoms, and their fragrance was heavy on the full breeze. She thought she might walk down into the yard to see Vera's plantings, but before she got down the steps, she heard the screen slam again and there was Mabel, carrying a second tray.

"Here we is. Mint julep time." She set the tray down. This one had a tall, sweating glass filled with crushed ice, and topped with sprigs of mint.

"From the garden." Mabel offered it after she helped Grace settle in.

"My goodness, Mabel. That didn't take long."

"Well, I had another tray ready."

"Ready?"

"Well, you know, I was thinkin' maybe you'd be wantin' somethin' more than the lemonade."

"So you had this all prepared ahead of time." Grace considered the circumstances enchanting, considering Vera was so dyed-in-the-wool about what was proper and what wasn't.

"I got a whole pitcher in there, just waitin' to be drunk. And I do mean drunk."

"Where's yours?"

"Oh, ma'am, I—"

"Surely, you don't think I'm going to drink alone. You know, Mabel, if there's one thing I do remember, it's that a lady never drinks alone. Please, join me. Please."

"I did do everything there is to do inside…"

"Well then, you've earned your reward. Go on, into the house, and get yourself a glass."

Mabel left again, and Grace closed her eyes and listened to the distant parade music. There was no way to escape the streams of sound that traveled up and over buildings, down overgrown lanes, and onto the porches.

There was another creak, then a slap of the screen door. Mabel was back, with sheepish smiles. She joined Grace, standing uneasily by the white wicker settee.

"Now, Mabel," Grace admonished, "how can we have a proper visit when you won't sit down?"

"Too use'ta waitin on other people." Mabel shrugged. "Just don't feel right sittin', doin' nothin."

Grace raised her glass. "I want to propose a toast. To Mabel, who runs the house, and looks after everyone. Without whom nothing would go smoothly. Sit down, Mabel." She gestured. "Make yourself comfortable. I'd love to hear some stories about the good old South. Vera tells stories about the South, but her stories are so very boring, you know."

"Don't say?"

"Absolutely. I can't figure out whether my good friend has no creative imagination, or whether she's just led a sheltered life. For instance—"

The conversation continued. Barriers were broken, and the two went on to form a secret bond that neither could explain, but both knew existed.

"Tell me about your life in New Orleans, Mabel. Have you always lived here with your family?"

"My family lived here when we was slaves and worked the cotton fields for the masters. Later on, we did it on our own. We was workers for pay."

"So, your family roots go far back in this region."

"Way, way back, ma'am. Way back. We seen things here—you people ain't known nothin' about."

"What kinds of things?"

Mabel hesitated, and Grace persisted.

"Really. Tell me. This may be the last time I have to learn anything new."

Mabel looked soulfully at Grace, then down at her lap.

"Oh, it's all right, Mabel. I'm not afraid of what's ahead. I feel I've had a good life, and I can't complain. I have a husband who loves me—"

"No children?" Mabel interrupted. This seemed important to the earnest-looking woman who held her glass tightly in labor-roughened hands. Grace shook her head.

"No children, I'm afraid. I was a spoiled little debutante. I bloomed late in life, was surrounded by protection of one sort or another until my late twenties, and wasn't permitted to just go out with friends. Or to make my own, for that matter. My friends were all chosen for me."

Again, Mabel shook her head. "Nasty way to grow up, if you ask me."

"When I met Mr. Henning, I was well on my way to becoming an old maid. Oh, I could have managed very well financially. When my parents died, with little Joel having been dead for so many years, I was the sole beneficiary of all that my parents left. But I was lonely."

"Yes, ma'am. Can be lonely, just one lady like you all alone in a big house. You live up by that racetrack, Miz Vera say."

"Yes I do. But I want you to tell me about New Orleans, won't you?"

"I will, but you gotta say which things you wanta hear, Miz Henning."

The unlikely couple settled in, and Mabel told stories about the rising tides that threatened the city below sea level, so that even the cemeteries were built above ground. She said they built huge stone mausoleums that were monuments to the spirits of New Orleans. Mabel shifted from that topic to voodoo, explaining that she'd had a niece who practiced the art.

"So you really believe in it, the art of voodoo?"

"You believe in it, if you know what's good," Mabel said in a low voice, eyes shifting sideways. "Been too many things happened not to believe in it. People like you—no offence, ma'am—but people like you think voodoo is funny. They come in to New Orleans, drink at the jazz places, and buy baby voodoo dolls fa' souvenirs. They don't know shit 'bout what they'ze messin with—'scuze me, Miz Henning."

"No, no. Go on," Grace prompted, eyebrows raised. "I agree with you one-hundred percent." She dabbed the corner of her mouth with the white linen napkin Mabel had left on the tray, and nodded enthusiastically. "Do, go on. I find this very educational, Mabel."

Sometime later, Mabel clutched her cloth handbag, bid Mrs. Henning good night, and sauntered on her way. Both were fairly well intoxicated, but Mabel explained she had only a short walk home.

"But, do be careful," Grace warned. "After everything you've told me, I don't want you to be eaten by any of those voodoo witches."

Mabel laughed and shook her head. "You is somethin' else, Miz Henning. You still don't get it. But I guess it don't matter. I guess you don't hafta."

Grace strolled about the yard, unable to resist the azaleas and the bougainvillea. She decided to enjoy the porch and garden, and forget about going back inside. The sun was going down. It was darker in the garden than it had been. When she'd filled her lungs with fragrance, she stepped back onto the porch, fanning her face with a Mardi Gras program she'd found on the table in the foyer. Grace looked closer at the paper she held in her hand: *A Guide To Mardi Gras*. The leaflet described the whys and wherefores of the Carnival, the streets filled with larger-than-life floats and the fueled torches that were the source of light for the parade. There were the colors of Mardi Gras, gold and purple and green. They stood for health, wealth, and wisdom.

"Flambeaux," Grace said aloud, sounding like a schoolgirl learning her vocabulary. "Flambeaux. Mardi Gras. Lundi Gras—"

Grace sighed and decided that solitude wasn't really such a bad friend. She sat for endless moments stretching seamlessly, one into another, lulled by the comforting creak of the rocker on the wide-planked wooden floor. Rocking and rocking, back and forth, the breeze running over her face in measured doses until she almost slept.

Sometime later, she roused with a start and noticed the shapes of things were getting harder to see. She decided on one more foray into the courtyard to get a closer look at some of Vera's plantings. Grace picked her way into the garden, listing and swaying. The overpowering colors around her, the vibration from the music, and heavily perfumed gardenias made her dizzy. She had to walk along slowly, leaning against the trees for support. A minute later, the wind picked up with an undercurrent moan.

Grace buttoned the top two buttons of the soft cardigan sweater she wore over the lounging pajamas, turned on her heels, and stepped further along. She halted in her tracks, stung by the fact that she was alone, and wished fleetingly that she had gone to the parade. The premonition of a storm sent her back in the direction of the porch. She wondered if she should go inside to shut the windows, draw the curtains, and pull the shades. The wind died instantly, as though it had read her thoughts and wanted her to stay. Somehow she couldn't bring herself to leave the beautiful spot, bathed in moonlight. It was a feast for the senses, and she lingered in spite of the darkness. How wonderful to be in New Orleans. More than any other place on earth, she was glad to be here. Grace reached for a white rose and plucked one of its petals. She rubbed it between thumb and forefinger, examining it close up. Its scent lingered on her fingers. It was the softest thing she'd ever felt; she was lost in the sensation.

And then, somewhere further along the path, a twig snapped. Grace took a few steps forward, peering to see from where the sound had come. At first, she saw nothing, but then a figure stepped out from behind a thicket.

It wore a costume of shiny triangles, gold and green and purple. The player had donned a three-pronged hat with bells at the ends, and his eyes were masked. It was as if an icon from the Mardi Gras had come to life. Grace blinked hard, squinting at the image. Then, suddenly, the head-piece moved and the tiny bells' silvery ring carried on the wind, giving birth, making it real.

Grace spun sideways, retreating quickly toward the safety of the front porch. She tripped up two of the steps, then spun around to look behind her. The costumed fig-ure had followed, slipping along the cobblestone walkway, one ballet-like step in front of the other. Without a word, without a sound except for the bells. He almost seemed a figment, but the vision of purple and green burned indel-ibly, pinpricks of light in the dim. The darkened figure paused on his way, reaching up with graceful hands to pick a rose from the overhead arbor that joined the house lawns to the garden. His every movement was liquid magic.

Grace backed up the steps, half amused, half alarmed, as the animated charm scaled the rail and hopped over it. It met her on the porch. Grace fell back onto the swing. She gasped as the harlequin knelt and gently reached for her hand. He raised it to his red-painted lips and kissed... then laid the flower across her lap. In the single moment suspended in time, she caught a glimmer in his eye, noticed the painted teardrop on his cheek. It was blue, not an ocean blue or a navy, but indigo. Deeper than the blanket of darkness around them. The jester trotted down the stairs and disappeared in the courtyard.

*

Martha looked at Simon. "A wayward harlequin in purple silk, bells jingling—blocks from the parade. When she told them about it later, the Whitworths were thrilled. They thought the whole incident was enchanting. Nobody paid much attention. It was a random event. It wasn't until later that I diagnosed the occurrence as Grace's first hallucination."

Simon groaned, and shook his head consolingly. "But you weren't to know that at the time."

"No. All I knew was that she really needed to be settled in, so that when she had problems, she'd already be in the system. It's difficult to wait until everything is falling apart and then try to transfer documents, sign papers, et cetera."

Simon shifted in his seat. "Of course, there's another way to look at it, Martha. You could let your patient live in normal surroundings and bring in added resources as you needed them. That'd be one way to maintain normalcy in the setting she lives in."

"Don't second-guess me, Simon. John had made it clear he didn't trust in-home health care." She bristled. "There are half a dozen ways to do it. I chose one. That's my job. She had a husband who was away at work more often than not, and a housekeeper who was paid to clean the house, not to care for Mrs. Henning. Her husband was not comfortable leaving her at home when he wasn't there."

"Well, that's true," Simon concurred. "And what was done was perfectly within acceptable standards."

"Just not what you would have done."

"Maybe not. I might have brought in an aide of some kind, to make the process more gradual. A lot of this depends on what kind of support you get from the family of the patient."

"And that's why I did what I did. Mr. Henning had told me that he worked long hours and the help they had was there just for domestic chores. I felt he wanted her cared for, and I admitted Grace when I did in an effort to comply."

"Okay. All right." Simon pushed away from the desk. "I'm just asking, Martha. I have a right to do that." He'd held himself tightly in all morning; sealing in the emotion that ate away at him. Now the strain was showing, and he was beginning to lose his temper. His legs were stiff, his mind numb, and he was baited by the prospect of breathing fresh air and seeing the trees. She, in the meantime, had fallen silent, though she watched him with trained eyes, as if sensing too that it was time to stop. An errant lock of his hair fell forward as he bent over the file, scribbling something across the top of the page.

"How much do we need to cover?" she asked.

Simon let out a heavy sigh. "I think we've covered enough." He turned to her, and his forceful tone belied a tender expression. "I want you to go home, Martha. Don't think about this. We have plenty of time. We can get together in a few days, and cover the period after she came to live at the institute."

"Is there anything you want me to bring next week that you don't have now?"

Simon considered the question, wanted to say no; to tell her to relax and get her sleep.

"Just see if you can put together your impressions for me. Taking the records for what they say is an objective approach. But I know that you made most of your decisions based on something more intangible. I do it too. So, go home, and see if you can't put down on paper what influenced you at the time. This is the type of thing that may be invaluable."

He said it grudgingly, not wanting to admit, even to himself, that it may come to that. The meeting over, Martha asked, "What are the chances?" They stood only a few feet apart in the quiet office. Simon shook his head and looked away. He couldn't hold out false hope.

"You aren't optimistic," she volunteered.

"Give me what I need to prove you're the good doctor I know you are." With that he stepped closer, eyes resting on her lips. He turned away with effort and walked to the door, opening it. "I'll see you next week."

Chapter 6

HENRY'S CAR WAS NOT in the lot. Maybe he'd be late, though Simon's friend was punctual as a rule.

The handsome storefronts caught Simon's eye. How long had it been since he'd gone shopping? He honestly couldn't remember. A woman inside the store window tucked a purple scarf inside the neck of a long white coat. The mannequin wore it well. She struck a haughty pose, one-foot forward, hand on hip.

He thought about how Martha would look in the coat, with heavy gold earrings and some kind of boots. She would look smashing. And, he knew she would wear incredible perfume. Like the old days.

He strolled along past each window, hands in his pockets. He'd walk to one end of the trendy shopping center, then turn back and look for Henry. A door opened and the sweet smell of chocolate wafted past. He found himself wandering in, buying coffee and chocolates, as if filling his hands with them would fill the emptiness in his heart. Then, exiting the shop, he glanced curiously down at his arms. Why had he bought chocolate? He never ate candy. Martha probably still liked it. The thought popped into his head. What if he was out buying things for her? What would it be like to get into his car and drive over to her house for coffee?

The critical half of his brain flashed an alert, telling him it was a foolish and pointless idea. Leave it alone, it warned.

He passed an art gallery. The plate glass gleamed, and the rich texture of canvas and swirling colors leaped out at him. There was a landscape in a gold gilt frame. The under-painting gave it a glow, as if from the sun, and he wondered how it was done, with tiny blobs of pigment and fine sable brushes. It was an early spring scene, trees budding, just after a rain.

The artist had done a terrific job. Simon pulled his coat collar up; could almost feel the droplets sliding down his neck. In his mind's eye he saw a young Martha with an armload of books, smiling up at him. And him, stealing glances at her. In the beginning, just feeling her out, to see what the undercurrent was, if there might be something between them. And there was, months later, when she'd finished her psychiatry rotation and they had no official connection. The chemistry had been there. She'd known it too. There were times she seemed to fight it, going out of her way to avoid him. As if she didn't trust herself.

Simon studied the ellipse of a puddle in the painting in the window. It reflected the sky so beautifully. And he remembered the day they had all been caught in the rain at the interns' picnic. It came down hard. Everybody scurried for cover, scooping up dirty plates and used cups. Martha stood on a table, just under the eaves of the pavilion. She was pulling down a handful of balloons. He knew she was going to fall even before she started to teeter. He came up from behind, lunged forward, and caught her as she crashed to the soaking ground. And he went with her, trying to cushion the fall by pivoting and bringing her down on top of him.

She turned a bright red, and pushed back and up from his chest, green eyes wide, bangs dripping.

"Doctor Talbot!"

"Simon," he said quietly, inches from her face.

"Simon." And something in the way she spoke said that it was the beginning.

She came to him often after that, to seek his advice, and sometimes when there was no reason.

A man stopped next to him at the window to look at the oil, and Simon jolted back to the present. He decided he'd better head back to meet Henry.

*

The Irish pub had a heavy-with-wood feel in the bar, and strains of music came from a live band in the rear. The place had a spirited crowd. Folks came to shoot darts. There was a toy box in an area where families sat to eat. It was down home, with hearty food and a friendly atmosphere.

Simon spent the first few moments just standing inside the doorway, adjusting to the dim light, looking around inside for his old schoolmate. Henry sat just off from the bar, inside a small area carved out for a bay window. Here you could see passersby. Simon stood over Henry, who watched a woman and a boy loading bags into the trunk of their car. The lad looked happy.

"Toys, do you think?" Simon asked, and slid into the seat opposite his friend.

"Oh, there you are. I didn't see you come in." Henry shook with laughter, then leaned over and squeezed his friend's arm. "How are you? I've missed you."

Simon considered before answering. "I'm sorry I haven't called in a while."

He smiled at the waitress who nodded, then promptly delivered two mugs of stout to their table where, by that time, they were already engaged in heavy conversation.

"So, he's walking the three-and-a-half blocks— whatever it is, to get to the hospital, you see, and he thinks he's had a heart attack," Henry said. "He isn't sure, but he says he felt he was having an attack. In his chest. And that's a reliable assumption. Now, my client went looking for help and headed for the hospital."

"Why did he walk? Why not take a cab?"

"There weren't any."

"In Syracuse?"

"Maybe he couldn't find one. He had to walk."

"You don't have to prove it to me, Henry; tell it to the jury. Those people are going to want to know why he walked three blocks to a hospital. And if I don't ask the question, you can be sure they will."

"Try looking at it from a different angle. From my perspective, a person doesn't have to have good reasons for doing things until he breaks the law. Arguably, it wasn't the best idea in the world, but it was his choice. It's a free country…" Henry waited.

"Well, all right…" Simon chaffed irritably.

"You're getting hung up on a moot point. This man, my client, came limping into the Emergency Room for treatment. He was allowed to stand there, without a wheelchair, without being led to a gurney—nothing—until he keeled over."

"Oh, God."

"Well, hang on. That's not the worst of it. Not only was he, in fact, having a heart attack, but he broke his hip in the fall. This is a man on steroids. Any idea what that stuff does to your bones? It melts them."

Simon drew a long, thirsty draft from his mug. He set the glass down, gave an audible sigh, and turned to his friend. "I have a vague idea of what steroids can do."

"Sorry, of course you do. So, don't you agree, that the inattention from the ER staff was—"

"I don't agree with anything. Counsel is leading the witness; putting words in his mouth. You can't do that. I know. I grew up on Perry Mason."

"So did I."

"Then don't waste the court's time."

Henry leaned back and squinted at his drinking buddy. "You're in a bad mood today."

"Am I?"

"What is it?"

Simon said nothing.

"You can tell me." Henry leaned forward, with earnest appeal.

"Sorry. I've been investigating a case for a medical board hearing that involves someone I used to care about."

The comment hung, suspended in midair. Henry turned serious. "And still do, I would guess…"

That was the go-ahead. Henry, expert counselor that he was, slowly but carefully dragged every detail out of his friend. Though the two hadn't seen each other for months, they picked up where they'd left off. Simon told Henry about the precarious spot he was in.

"How do you plan to handle it, Simon?"

"I'll get all the facts."

"Right."

"I'll review them, set against the different criteria."

"Good."

"Then, I'll decide the case."

"Just like that." Henry lowered his voice; conspiring across the table. "Let me make it easy for you, old boy. You're falling for this woman all over again. You didn't learn a thing the first time she sent you packing."

"It wasn't like that. First of all, we never lived together. And we never actually…consummated…"

"Had sex."

"I didn't say that."

"You couldn't. You're much too decent."

"Why are you browbeating me like this?"

"I?" Henry balked, incredulous. "We've been friends for a very long time. And we should be able to tell each other the truth. Unless we don't know it ourselves."

"What's that supposed to mean?" Simon scowled over at his friend, shifting uncomfortably.

"You should see yourself," Henry laughed. "You're glaring at me."

"Well, I'm sorry. You think I don't know what's going on in my own life."

"Sometimes that happens, even to psychiatrists."

"And I suppose you have the answers that will save me."

A little grin played at the corners of Henry's mouth.

"Oh, come on, Simon. It's easy to see you're head over heels for her. At least to me. Why don't you recognize it? Admit it, so you can move on."

Simon brooded, deep in his quandary.

"In the end, you'll either go back with her, or walk away," Henry persisted. "So, which is it?"

Simon stared off. "I don't know," he said quietly.

"May I ask why you two separated in the first place?"

There was a long moment, when Simon didn't answer. Couldn't. "I suppose we were both too driven. With our careers. She had yet to make her mark on the world, and she wanted to do that. Medical school and internship take up your life. There really isn't time for anything or anybody else."

"Tell that to your married colleagues."

"It's rough for them. And, maybe it was hard too, being a woman in a male-dominated field. She couldn't afford to make mistakes. All eyes were on her. I don't know. Something like that. It's supposition. I never said, 'Why can't you and I be together?' When I sensed that she wasn't interested in more than what we had; I backed off, that's all."

"What did you have, exactly?"

"Well, we had friendship, and the student-teacher thing. But I'll tell you, this inquiry is killing me. I want to protect her and I don't know if I'm going to be able to."

"Sounds to me like you ought to withdraw from the case."

"I can't. She'd be at the mercy of whoever succeeded me." Simon finished the last of his stout, and set down the empty glass with a note of finality. "Tell me about that poor fellow with the heart attack."

"He's doing fine. But we're suing the hell out of the hospital."

"Ouch. I don't want to hear the rest. Just remember that you were talking about intentions just a little while ago. A man can do what he wants until he breaks the law, so long as he has the right intentions. What about the hospital? They didn't set out to aggravate this guy's condition."

"Negligence," Henry stated.

"Negligence."

Chapter 7

IMPRESSIONS. THAT'S WHAT he wanted. Martha had thoughts about Simon too, recalling the picture of a soft curl hanging down over his forehead. She wanted to go home, put her feet up with something cold to drink, and savor them. But Grace came first, and she needed a clear head for that. What had impressed her in the beginning?

Once inside her apartment, she wasted no time getting to work. She pulled a chair up to the rolltop desk in her study, chose a pen from the pencil caddy, and decided that a longhand account put her more in touch with her subject. She wished she'd spent more time observing the smaller details over those last few months, but daily life had only taken on the significance it does, lackluster and mundane. Now, it was time to recall those fine details. They were details she feared—

if she thought back and tried to remember—might not be there at all…

*

Grace sat down below, on the first floor in the glass-walled solarium. She was playing cards with three other women. They were neat, smart women with newly coifed hairstyles and expensive jewelry. Manicured hands held the cards. Bridge.

Martha turned to Mr. Henning. "I'm glad you could come. I wanted to bring you up to date."

"Yes, of course." John Henning held his silk tie to his chest as he bent forward and sat down. He looked briefly over the rail of the observation deck, down onto the scene below where Grace sat oblivious to them, chatting, shuffling through her hand of cards.

"Do you usually observe them from above like this?"

Martha laughed and blushed, slightly embarrassed. "Oh, no. No. We wouldn't ever do that—watch them secretly. This second deck is for the use of residents to look down over the palms and the ferns planted in the sunroom." Martha looked at her guest. "I wish you wouldn't be so automatically suspicious of our methods, Mr. Henning."

"I didn't mean to sound accusatory, doctor."

"It's all right. But I want you to know that the staff wouldn't do that. We're just not that devious."

She looked below, and saw Grace flip a frothy scarf over one shoulder, then redistribute her cards, smiling at the others.

"Fair enough." He smiled, but the smile did nothing to reach his eyes.

"It's a good sign that your wife wanted to play bridge. She can make friends here."

Henning sat silent.

"Those others are from the East Wing," Martha offered, and still he said nothing. "Look, I know it's hard, but it's the best thing. For Grace. You can spend as much time as you like with her. Take her home on weekends if you want to. She won't be a prisoner here."

"Tell me, Dr. Reed, didn't you say that you were impressed with Grace's mini-travelogue of New Orleans?"

"Well, yes—"

"Did you not say that?"

"Yes, I did, but I don't see—"

"It's hard for me to think ahead, I suppose. Can't quite bring myself to believe she wouldn't have been able to live at home much longer. I mean, how could this woman, and the woman who gave you an armchair tour of the City of New Orleans, be one and the same?"

Martha was wary of reasoning with him.

"You describe a woman on the verge of collapse," he said.

"Inevitably, she will regress, Mr. Henning."

"It's so hard to think it will happen soon."

"She may have definite ideas about what she wants for herself, and I think she's fully capable—now, anyway—of grasping what's happening to her, and what's likely to happen. Have you sat with her and really talked about her illness?"

"Is that what you want me to do?"

"Yes."

*

Martha flexed stiff fingers. Writer's cramp. She ignored the stiffness. The particulars were coming so easily now that she forced herself to forge ahead, and to think back. What were her impressions?

There was a pattern to life within the halls of Helsey. It was a private institution that catered to people who could afford to be there. They were residents, not patients. Care had been taken to avoid a regimented look, from the grounds around Helsey to the dress code within. It had been decided long ago that uniform dress would negatively affect not only the residents, but also the staff indirectly. If people were allowed their individuality, then it would be something honored, even cherished.

Martha thought about the role she'd played in establishing Helsey's policies. She liked to think she'd affected hospital practice. The stereotypic gothic buildings and dark-age technology that stuck in the public consciousness for sanitarium settings weren't always too far from the truth. In medical school she'd studied the archaic methods used at the onset of her field, and shivered at the thought of them; visions of Bedlam with its straw-covered galleries, the hopeless insanity that coalesced and dripped from the walls. Stoic, brawny caretakers blocking the halls and running the building with pea-sized intellect.

Martha kept that genesis in mind when she fought for the freedoms of those being treated, cutting restrictions and mandates down to the necessary few.

And there were other aspects not considered important, that had to do with the mental climate of the treatment center. Martha saw it as a whole. One aspect, however small, would affect the entire asylum. This meant lush landscaping and elaborate plantings on the grounds around the buildings. It was a dense and secluded enclave. Where other staff members had campaigned to level the land, and install extra parking, Martha insisted that this was home for the inpatients, and that they deserved more than vistas of concrete.

Martha smiled faintly. She had known that Grace would test the rules. Grace moved in, along with a dozen trunks of clothing. Dresses and skirts with silk blouses. Blazers, smart wool slacks; Gucci shoes and handbags. Martha felt compelled to protect Grace from the censure she was bound to face when forced to coexist with other long-established residents.

She poked her head in, to see Grace laying out her clothes on the queen-size bed she had brought in from home. The bed was a showstopper. Rosewood; dark red-brown and heavy with intricate carvings. Animal claw feet and flowers intertwined with symbols of colonialism; pineapples capped each post. This was Grace Henning. This was her room, and that was that.

Martha knocked.

"Yes?" Grace swung around, bright eyed. "Dr. Reed! You're just in time. I told them I might need more closet space. I'm not sure I can fit everything in."

She seemed excited, as if anticipating the move like a new college student, freshly liberated from home.

"I wanted to be all settled before Monday, so I could concentrate on our sessions." She might just as easily have said "lessons," as Martha had the feeling Grace saw Helsey as a temporary circumstance.

"You probably will want to separate everything by season: at least cold weather and warm weather," Martha suggested.

"Oh, yes, absolutely," Grace agreed, scooping up arm-fuls of sweaters and dividing them into piles.

"We have a fairly simple lifestyle here," Martha offered. "You'll have meals in the dining room, and sessions in my office or wherever we decide to set up for that particular day. Then, there are other, social events; the small parties and activities. You can pick and choose which ones of those you're interested in. And, when someone comes to visit you, and you want to go out somewhere, you'll need clothes for that."

She had tried to be helpful, and Grace was appreciative. In the end, they'd settled on a simple, basic wardrobe, and Martha convinced Grace to send some of it back.

The jewels were another matter altogether. Grace had brought with her an assortment of pearls; necklaces of varying lengths, bracelets, rings and earrings. There were pendants of semi-precious jewels, no doubt what Grace would consider casual accessories, with the stones in some of the pendants eight carats or more. And rings, flanked with sapphires and emeralds, and dangling earrings studded with diamonds.

"I wanted to be able to accessorize," was Grace's explanation. Martha understood how, on the outside, in another place, at another time, this would all be perfectly reasonable. But this was Helsey. No matter what had gone before, life would be a faded copy of what Grace B. Henning had always known. Only Mr. Henning's adamant insistence and his agreement to sign a release made it possible for Grace to keep her jewelry with her. He felt it would make her happy.

*

Martha left Grace's apartment, pausing to take a long look before she left. This room would never be the same. Grace would transform it into a grand salon. She'd have it ready to receive royalty in a few days. Martha bid Grace good-bye and closed the door slowly behind her. Maybe this was going to be all right after all. Just maybe, Grace would somehow settle in. Mr. Henning had his reservations about the idea, but then again, who wouldn't? Any loving husband would rebel against the prospect of locking his spouse away in an institution, no matter how fine the furnishings. Then too, he didn't want her at home, at the mercy of an unknown aide from an agency...well, there was no perfect solution, was there?

Martha walked further down the hall. Forrest Greeley's door was open as she passed. Helsey's chief administrator was sitting at his desk.

"Oh, Dr. Reed. May I see you for a moment?"

Martha obliged, grudgingly. She'd never liked Greeley. His office was an interior decorator's standard portfolio. The colors were the perfect compliments on the color wheel. Yellow-violet, green-red. Everything in order, with the obvious strained effort of an amateur who thinks he's doing everything right. Bookends matched perfectly, twin chairs, double bookshelves. Obsessive. Compulsive. Greeley obviously never had an autonomous thought in his life.

"Close the door, will you, doctor."

She did as she was asked, though it seemed unnecessary under any circumstances. She spoke first, determined to take the initiative. "Yes. What can I do for you, Mr. Greeley?"

He motioned for her to sit, but she ignored the gesture. Let him say his piece. She didn't plan to spend any length of time in the administrator's office, closed door or not.

"Have you installed Mrs. Henning?" he wanted to know.

Like a dishwasher, she thought. "She's installed and running fine. Is there a problem?"

"I certainly hope not," Greeley sniffed. "If there are any problems, I will be notified immediately, is that clear?"

Martha stood, mute against the door, arms folded. Who did he think he was talking to?

"Dr. Reed," he began, sounding conciliatory. "I've been at the Institute for fifteen years now. I see so many people come and go, and my main objective is, of course, to see that the Institute remains in good health financially. Your objective has to do with the mental health and well-being of the residents."

"Your point?" She didn't feel like being civil to this man.

"Just this, Dr. Reed. Due to the current Medicare and Medicaid laws in this state, the Institute must house a great many patients—residents," he corrected himself, "who would not otherwise be able to stay here. We take them in; sometimes they have the necessary funds, sometimes not, but we take them all in. And when they run out of money, the law prohibits us from removing them. They continue to stay."

"Yes," she said. "It really is too bad we can't just throw them out on the street."

"That is not what I mean, Dr. Reed. The fact is that few people can afford to pay their own way. Mrs. Henning is one of the few. And I will not have her husband pulling her out of here because things aren't going splendidly, is that clear?"

"Why on earth would you approach me with this?"

"Because you are her doctor."

"Do you have some problem with the way I practice medicine, Mr. Greeley?"

"Not at all."

"Then forgive me," she said, pulling the door open impatiently. "I'm really much too busy to continue this conversation." With that, she left. People were always kissing up to Greeley. She wasn't going to be one of them.

*

Martha settled back. She watched Simon rifle through the yellow lined pages of a notepad. He said little; just a nod, a grunt, and an occasional screwing up of his lips when he came to something he was having trouble digesting. She did nothing to interfere. Then he put the pad down, carefully, squinting at some invisible point. "Would you say she settled in well?"

"She did with the help of the staff, and there was a fair degree of acceptance by the others. The group she associated with were, after all, moneyed people, caught short by the inconvenience of their illnesses and placed at Helsey."

"Is that how you see it, Martha? 'Caught short by inconvenience'?"

"They didn't succumb to sickness. They were used to better, Simon."

"What does that mean, exactly, Martha?"

"Just what I said."

"Forgive me for saying so, but you're beginning to sound a little elitist. Not the idealist I took to the hill-towns of North Carolina."

"I'm just stating the facts. In the world, you have people who are poor and underprivileged, and people who are very fortunate. And Helsey was filled, in most part, with a privileged minority. What do you want from me, Simon? What's wrong with that?"

"What'd you get out of that summer, anyway, Martha? Anything?"

She was seized by the question, off-guard, defensive. "I got quite a lot out of it. It might surprise you, but I formed some everlasting beliefs about what I do and why I do it."

"Good."

"What?"

"I said, good. I'm relieved to know that at the very least, you noticed a difference between the "have's and the have-nots."

"What the hell is your problem?"

"I beg your pardon, young lady?"

"You heard me. What are you trying to prove? This isn't about Grace Henning and what happened to her at Helsey. It's about you and your ego. You want me—or you wanted me—to follow in your footsteps as the bleeding heart of medicine. You'd gladly spend the remainder of your career in some dusty, disease-infested camp in a third world country, and you know it."

"Sounds like an indictment. Assuming that were true, I suppose I should be ashamed of my motives."

"No, no! You twist my words around. What do you want from me?" She was up and out of her seat, approaching his desk, the only barrier between them.

Simon held her at bay with raised palms. "Wait. Sit down. Please, Martha. Sit down."

She did as she was told.

"Deep breath...I'm sorry, Martha. I'm sorry." He shifted and swiveled sideways, his attention grabbed by the seagoing vessel going down. "Now, let's back up, and start over. I don't mean to antagonize you in any way. This is simply my way, however clumsy, to get at the substance of the issues. I don't know what these people want. I've never been called upon by the board to take part in an inquest like this. So give me a break, will you?"

She was calmer now. "All right." She crossed her legs.

Simon noticed her skirt hiking up a few inches with the movement and again looked away. He cleared his throat. "What I'd like to know is this: What did you yourself witness as Grace was settling in? What did you see, and was it in line with your expectations?"

"Well…Mary Hadley comes to mind."

"Mary—H-A-D-L—?"

"E-Y. Mary was another resident. Agoraphobic or something, I don't know. Don't hold me to it; she wasn't my patient. I knew Mary as a timid little thing. She was sliding along inside Helsey, perfectly at home. Mary's salvation lay in being saved from the outer world. She never felt safe there, even on the trips across the street that the van took to the discount department store. Mary could never handle them."

"You know a lot about her."

"I didn't treat her. But I saw plenty of her in the course of the day. Everybody saw Mary as something of an outcast. The residents, not the staff…"

"Well, I should hope not." Simon smiled dryly.

"But I think Grace saw Mary for the person she was inside. I introduced her to Mary. I took her up and down the hall to meet the people living in the East Wing, and Mary was one of them. Grace adopted her and I saw the two of them in the assembly room one morning, about a month after Grace came to stay. Mary was a bit shy, but Grace wasn't about to let that stand in the way."

"So, Mary seldom went outside, is that true, because of the agoraphobia?"

"Right."

"Did Grace try to get Mary to go out?"

"No, why?"

"Just wondering if Mrs. Henning was capable of appreciating Mary's condition—not her condition so much as her limitations. But you say, no. They were good for each other, in other words."

"Yes. Very good. In fact, there was a time when Mary signed up for a trip with Grace. They went to the opera. I can give you the details—you'd think her agoraphobia would have kicked in, but with Grace's prodding, Mary was a different person—not symptomatic at all in the ways she'd usually manifest."

"Wait. We'll get to that, but first your impressions about Grace herself, and how she adapted to the Institute. Is there anything in particular that sticks out in your mind?"

*

The first big event that Grace was present for at Helsey was a party. It was early spring and the grand theatre of the sanitarium was the scene for the lively get-together. Here was a space used for lectures and classes, but that night it was transformed to entertain the residents and friends of Helsey.

The grand theater, of spiral staircases and velvet runners was a last vestige of another era, the sole standing survivor from the days when Helsey was established. It was pre-World War I construction: an age of opulence, when the world had not yet drawn up stakes and started bombing. Most of the buildings had been renovated since then, and been given the stamp of high tech society, but not the grand theater. Some said that psychiatrists spent their free time there, to escape the times, and the madness.

Grace came down the velvet-covered stairway like a model on a runway in green silk, taking each lithesome step with careful precision. She was a vision, a beauty whose aura was mystery and drama, and Martha thought of Greta Garbo and Joan Crawford.

All wore party attire, though Grace stood out among them. Before long, she had become the center of attention and she reveled in it as everyone crowded around her. She looked radiant in her gown, trailing wisps of gauzy organza. Hers was one of the most stunning collections of clothing Martha had ever seen, and the staff had taken to calling her "duchess."

Martha noted that Grace seemed to like this, though Martha suspected that once, Grace would have been insulted by it. And Grace was still playing hostess, ladling punch into cups for the others, acting as if the party was her own.

But this was Helsey, and that made it sad and pitiful. Martha turned from the crowd, embarrassed and ashamed. From what she knew of Grace's former life, and the sort of man that John Henning was, this spectacle was little more than a comical farce. Thank God he wasn't there that evening to see it. At least one could say that Grace had adjusted. As well as could be expected.

Martha and Grace established regular habits after the party, with therapy in the mornings and outings in the afternoons. "Work first, play later," Grace would say. She liked the hour or so they spent each morning, and had said so, more than once.

The van was commissioned to take residents to art museums, and to matinee performances of plays and the symphony.

One Sunday, Martha stopped by the office to pick up files for the coming week. When she left, she closed the door, not wanting to disturb the peaceful quiet at her end of the East Wing. It pleased Grace that Martha was close by.

"In case I need you," Grace had said. Martha smiled as she stepped along the soft carpet down the corridor, pausing before a room. She heard voices; Grace's and someone else. Mary Hadley. Infectious laughter, then, "Let's have a theme, Mary. Pearls."

"Pearls?"

"And maybe fans. We could carry them. It's *Madama Butterfly*, so fans would be terribly appropriate, don't you think?"

"I don't have a fan."

"Don't worry about that," Grace bantered. "I have plenty to go around. Bracelets and necklaces and rings… earrings too. But we need basic black dresses. Something with a classic design. I'm a size eight, and you seem slim enough to borrow one of mine."

"I couldn't do that—"

"Why ever not? What am I going to do with all of those clothes?"

"That would be nice of you, Grace."

"*Madama Butterfly*—what a glorious drama."

"I thought you said it was an opera?"

"Oh, it is! Goodness, you've never seen it. I'm so glad. You'll sit right next to me. And you'll love it. Absolutely and positively. It's a drama, because of the story line. It's a substantial opera, not one of those flimsy-whimsy, flutter-in-the-breeze kinds of stories. Those are nice too, of course, but this is a tragic love story, and you can't help but be devastated by the sadness of it."

Mary must have been thinking. The room was quiet, and then she asked, "Will we need tissues?"

"Yes, my dear. Boxes and boxes of them!"

"That's very kind."

"And I have a drawer full of beautiful silk stockings that actually came from our trip abroad. Pumps…" Grace thought aloud.

"Pumps." Mary repeated.

"Nothing too high. We can't wear flat shoes. They're completely unfeminine."

Martha smiled and looked down at her own brown flats. What Grace must think of her.

Chapter 8

"IS IT WHAT YOU wanted, Simon?"

"Some of it, yes. I took the last twenty-four hours to review what you've given me on this." He patted the yellow legal-sized tablet. "You've done a good job. Gave me a sense of how she'd adjusted." He nodded. "Now, tell me about the point where you noticed a decline, would you?"

"Mmm, that's hard to say." Martha crossed one leg over the other. Simon couldn't help but notice the fine contours of her thighs. He looked away, distracted beyond measure, and wished she'd wear longer skirts around him.

"It's almost impossible to tell. First, there's the realistic possibility that she hid some of the symptoms of deterioration but also, I may just not have noticed."

"Don't tell me that," Simon instructed.

"What?"

"Remember, I'm adjudicating this inquiry. If you say to me, that you may not have noticed, it might easily be construed as negligence, or ineptitude. On your part. You have to take a defensive posture."

"Sounds like nonsense to me." She was angry. She glared at him and spun out of her chair, moving toward the window. "What is this all about anyway, Simon? Why am I being made a scapegoat for an accident that could have happened anywhere? Is it because I may have made enemies of the Powers That Be because I petitioned for changes? I know this kind of thing probably does happen every day, somewhere, but why me?"

Simon never shifted position, but sat straight up behind the blotter, dotting his i's, crossing his t's.

"To ask 'Why me?' is to miss the point, Martha. Or to ignore it. Either way, it is happening to you. Like it or not, you have to deal with it. There are gray areas you need to hone in on, and give plausible reasons why all of your judgments were made with careful deliberation."

"All right. I will."

"For example, when did you get the sense, if you did, that she was incapable of good judgment? Did you ever come to that conclusion?"

"No, I thought her decisions were good ones. Her judgment was sound. The inability to distinguish reality from fantasy is something else."

"You mean, hallucinations?"

Martha turned from the window. "Exactly."

"Physically, what was your assessment after she entered Helsey?"

"Well, she…"

Martha squinted at a distant vision, conduit for the story. "One day there were signs of apraxia in Grace's left hand. It shook when she handed me a paper. I can picture it so clearly."

*

Grace Henning poured over an assortment of papers laid out on a countertop. The two women sat in the solarium, teacups in hand. Grace was wearing bifocals, and Martha noted she looked very official. She waited until all the sheets were piled neatly, and Grace gestured toward them. "These are lists of activities for all of us residents."

"Activities, you say?"

"It's a list that we propose. All of us."

"You've done a survey to find out what the residents want to do?"

"How they'd like to spend their time, yes, Dr. Reed. You know we aren't all old relics waiting to be stuffed and hung."

"No, no! Do you think that's how I feel about inpatients at Helsey?"

"Not you. But the rest of the staff seems to treat us as if we were some idle curiosity." Grace leaned forward with a bitter look. "Do you have any idea what these people think is appropriate entertainment?"

Martha wanted to laugh. She knew where her patient was headed.

"I and my friends are appalled at their attitude. These people are hiring magicians, circus acts, and horrible church choirs that can't carry a tune. And they expect us to be entertained. They take us for idiots! These aren't the kinds of things I wanted to see before I came here. What makes anyone think that we want this now?"

She had a point. How many times had Martha winced at the lineup of scheduled events for the residents? Granted, they had a few activities like the opera, but for the most part, the entertainment was second rate at best.

"I have here a list of demands from the other residents and myself. We insist on being able to choose our own entertainment, and the dispensing of resources for them."

Grace proffered a paper. It shook as she handed it over. Martha accepted the paper, scanned it, and noticed a change in Grace's handwriting. The brain was sending messages that weren't reaching their destination. Maybe Grace hadn't noticed. Maybe she had. Martha wouldn't mention it until Grace verbalized concern. She suspected the loss of coordination was more of an embarrassment than a physical hindrance, and would take great pains to assure Grace that it didn't compromise her appearance.

"I'll review this list. It falls outside of my domain, of course. I'm not in charge of recreation, and I haven't got much say in what they plan, or how they plan it. As far as dispensing the resources, the only way anyone could influence that would be through the types of activities there are."

"I suppose you're right." Grace looked deflated.

"But I'd encourage you to go ahead with this plan. Talk to the others, get a sense of what you'd propose in place of what exists now. Then drum up some support. I know you can do that, Grace."

Grace smiled with the implied endorsement.

"Bring the information back to me," Martha said. "I'll introduce you to Jane Sheehan. She's our coordinator. She'll be sympathetic, I know. Now, tell me how you've been feeling?"

"Fine."

"I've noticed you're having a little trouble walking, is that right?"

"I suppose. The bricks are uneven."

"My suggestion would be to wear flatter shoes. Just for walking." Martha remembered her comment about flat shoes being unladylike. "High heels are really impractical for walking. I know you love to walk."

But the reasoning fell on deaf ears. Grace stared into space. She was off somewhere far away, her eyes vacant.

"Have you been outside today?"

"I went—yes."

"Good. Exercise is important."

"I walk every day."

"Excellent. I can't overemphasize how important it is."

Then Grace repeated one line, a question that she had asked before. "Would you like to see the waterfall? It's very pleasant there."

Martha considered briefly. "Maybe we could do that some day soon. In fact, the day after tomorrow there's a break in my schedule."

"They should fix those stones there. The birdfeeder hanging from the white birch trees. You know where that is, doctor?"

"Are there broken pieces of stone near the feeders?"

"They should use sesame seeds. If you want to draw cardinals, and of course you can't have the blue jays. They're very hard to keep, because they're aggressive. They need a particular house. And if it doesn't suit them, they leave forever…"

Martha had no knowledge of any waterfall in the vicinity. But it had been a bad day for Grace, and she had gone right on with something else. So she let it drop, thinking that it was just a passing fancy.

*

Martha drank the coffee Simon offered. They agreed to stay on late in the day to fill in the blanks and name the nebulous things that somehow added up to make a case.

"Hungry?" Simon lifted his eyes as he bent forward, pouring cream into the china cup she balanced on her knee.

"No. Not at all."

He deposited the silver coffee urn back on its tray, took his place at the desk, and nodded for her to continue.

"Not long after, I came in to the office and was told by the head nurse that Grace had worn her sweater backwards. The nurse said that she came into the morning room, where some people were reading the paper and having breakfast served to them, and took a seat with her friends. The nurse was there in attendance as always, but she stayed out of the way. Grace was a little more agitated, nurse said, than usual. Bewildered and out of it, like she wasn't sure she was in the right place at the right time. Then the nurse saw the sweater. Picture her, waltzing in with gleaming hair and gold earrings, expensive stockings and a cashmere sweater. Backwards."

"Sure it was backwards?"

"Am I sure?"

"Was the nurse in attendance sure that the sweater was backwards?"

"Well, let's put it this way: it was the general consensus of opinion that it was backwards, because they all laughed at her."

Simon winced, and shook his head.

"Not her friends," Martha corrected. "From what I gather, they tried to shield her. But you know how cruel people can be. And it was a V-neck, so it dipped down in the back instead of in front."

"Okay." Simon looked pained. "Okay…" As if he wanted her to hurry past that point so he could stop feeling badly. Martha paused to consider that Simon had that kind of passion in his soul. He was a good man. She peered across at him, and saw what he wore that day, for the first time; saw his handsome jawline and the cloudy eyes. Haunted eyes. And for the first time in a long time, she wondered about him, instead of thinking about herself.

"So, what then?" he asked quietly.

Martha snapped out of it. "Well, I guess she was given some strange looks and there were wayward comments from the other residents. But her close friends stood up for her, as I said. There was some banter going back and forth between the critics, two elderly women who were very pleased to point out to her that she was 'backwards,' and Grace's cronies from the opera. When Grace looked down and saw what they were talking about, she rushed out of the room. And when they told me I thought, This is it. It had come a lot sooner than I expected. I wondered what to do."

"What'd you do?"

"A few choice members of the staff were called; those I felt could be trusted. They were told to be very careful. And I told them to check to see that she was zipped and buttoned, and dressed properly and appropriately. I made an executive decision to withhold the information from John Henning."

Simon sat up and took notice. Something indefinable told him this last comment was more telling than the incident itself. He cocked his head to one side, wondering.

"I was unwilling, or unable, to be the bearer of bad news. That afternoon I was sitting at my desk—"

"Wait, now. Just a minute. You say you made a decision not to tell Mr. Henning?"

Martha studied the hands in her lap. "Yes."

"Why would you do a thing like that?"

"Like what?"

"Withhold information from the spouse of a patient? It makes absolutely no sense."

"To me it did."

"How so?"

Martha looked up at him, perplexed.

"You can't justify keeping the lid on details of a patient's condition," Simon said.

"Just hear me out. He often came in to visit her and occasionally stopped by the office. The next time he did, I'd fill him in on how she was doing."

"You just figured it didn't matter that his wife was wearing her clothing backwards."

"Simon, I had planned to tell him at the very next visit. I wanted the few days interim to see if she'd do it again. Maybe it was a one-time thing. It might be the last time she did anything like that for the next six months. I didn't want to concern him for no good reason. Besides, what was there to do about it, anyway?"

"It's not the point."

"No, I know it isn't, but I did plan to talk about it. Among other things, but not with a sudden phone call."

Simon frowned and bit his lip. He just wasn't happy with it. No self-respecting doctor would withhold data. Certainly no student of his. His subconscious groped thin air. Shame on you, he thought, but never gave his thoughts away.

"So, when did you tell him? I assume you did tell him?"

"Of course I did."

"How did he take it?"

"Fine. In stride. Which has more to do with the way I told him than the fact that I told him."

"The jury's still out. You won't get me to approve the way you handled it."

She glared over across the shining mahogany desk where Simon's hands were folded, waiting. Why did he always make her feel like a naughty little girl? Why couldn't she, after all these years, stand up to him and act as an equal instead of a subordinate?

"Your approval doesn't concern me anymore, Simon. As I say, one afternoon Grace came to the office. She stood in the doorway, fiddling with the scarf she had tucked into her blouse."

"Was she properly dressed that day?"

"Oh, yes. As I had predicted, she never really lapsed a second time with her outfit. Maybe she was clear-headed enough not to; maybe the fear of being ridiculed was part of it. I don't know, but she never had another problem with what she wore."

"Was it time for therapy?"

"Not at all. It was after lunch. We had most of our sessions in the mornings and left the rest of the day for hospital rounds. I was finishing up the last of the day's dictation when she came in, and I put it aside and waved her into a seat. I turned off my machine and gave her my full attention. She was so happy, she was perky."

"Perky?" Simon was scribbling across the paper.

"She wanted to know, oh, how did she say it? 'Would you like to see the waterfall? It's very pleasant there.' Those were her exact words, and I saw that she used the same wording as before when she invited me, as though she were reciting them."

"She invited you to this place." His pen stopped. He waited.

"I had most of my dictations done. Everything was out of the way, and there was no excuse not to go with her."

"Except that you weren't obliged to go on an outing with a patient, unless you wanted to. I know you as the sort of person who would."

Martha threw herself back, torso slapping against the seat. She was weary of trying to exhume the details. What if memory didn't serve her? What if she gave it to him wrong? She labored to bring the incident back.

*

Grace was excited about the sojourn. She led the way, enthusiastically picking out the route, talking over her shoulder. She wore her walking shoes and stepped easily over piles of twigs, dancing her way along the path. Martha followed cautiously at first, then with energy to match Grace's own. They took tight turns and crossed obscure side trails before the final bend fanned out into a clearing. Martha learned, quite accidentally, that Grace had her own special track through the woods. They cut through the underbrush, along a passage Martha hadn't known existed, and she assumed it was a place that only Grace knew about. How on earth had she come this way, and how could it be that she knew it so well?

"There might be poison ivy," Grace cautioned. "I don't know. Sometimes there is. I hope you don't mind."

"No. As a matter of fact, it's really a nice change. I spend so much time in the office. You should take walks. The fresh air is the best thing for you." Martha made the affirmation with nothing to back it up. In actuality, she was wary. The happiness she felt for Grace, witnessing her carefree smile and playful step across this ground, was tempered by a looming warning, that somehow, it was all too autonomous for a lady who lived in a sanitarium.

They had come to the very outskirts of the grounds of Helsey, long past the place where the property was tended, and a gap in the fence allowed for just enough room for a person to squeeze through. Judging from what Grace told her, Martha guessed that she had come there many times before. The trail meandered on forever, erratic to the untrained eye, yet Grace advanced confidently, picking out the way.

The journey went on just long enough for Martha to have doubts. Just as better judgment was about to speak, they rounded a bend, and there it was. They looked down on a rocky crevice of cascading water, traveling in a gurgling trail down tumbling boulders. Grace halted, and turned with the spark of excitement in her eyes. She looked at Martha, to see if her vision was shared. It was.

The two sat along the hillside, feet dangling in the water. Two ordinary people, enjoying what nature had provided. Equals, or almost. And it was indeed, "very pleasant."

*

"So you'd made this discovery, of the falls." Simon looked pointedly at her, frowning.

"I made the discovery of the falls on that day. With no previous knowledge of its existence, and no real indication of how often she'd actually gone there, all I could do was go from there. Take it from that point and decide what importance it had."

"Well, it was clearly a spot that she enjoyed," Simon said. "A place she knew about already, and had introduced you to—what, because you were her doctor, or because she felt some affinity for you, as a friend?"

Martha paused, to sense his mood. Was this a trick question? Would he do that? "Does it make a difference?"

"Not to me. But, even if she let you in on it as a friend, you'd still be duty bound to regard the repercussions on her as your patient."

"I see. Well, I can tell you she brought me there. Who knows what she was thinking? I'd like, naturally, to assume it was because of our close relationship, which was more than as a doctor to her patient. But either way, I can only say that she insisted I come, that she'd mentioned it more than once, and that when I finally agreed, I discovered a delightful place. We took our shoes off and stepped onto the rocks until the water ran over our feet and our ankles, and we walked right underneath the falls."

"Didn't you get wet?" Simon accused.

"Well, as a matter of fact, we did."

Simon threw down his pen. He looked annoyed. "What were you thinking?"

"Just that Grace, who was her own person, had found a place that she went to for some solitude. And that she had finally decided to introduce me to it."

"Did she act as if she was afraid you'd disapprove in any way?"

"Of the falls?" Martha was doubtful.

"Yes. Did she give you the idea she knew she wasn't to go there?"

"No. She didn't. My distinct impression was that this was one of her private haunts and that she wanted to include me, so she did."

"And did there come a time when you informed the maintenance staff that the area around the fence was unstable, and that you wanted to make sure they secured it?"

"I returned to the office, if that's what you mean. I sat there, and the first thought that crossed my mind was what a wonderful afternoon we'd had. You know, I didn't even give a thought to anything else. Wasn't Grace entitled to an enjoyable afternoon at the falls the way you or I would go to the golf course?

"But then, after a little while, I did think about the safety factor. I wondered about that gap in the fence and whether the property was secure in the way it should have been. I would suggest that they install a gate that could be opened for supervised walks. But I wasn't worried about Grace wandering off."

"Despite the fact that wandering can be one of the elemental manifestations of Alzheimer's?"

"Not inevitably."

"But why take that chance?"

"She showed it to me. She knew the way, guided me there, and guided me back. She chose to take me there. Had it not been for her, I'd have been ignorant of the place's very existence."

"So what did you do then?"

"I had a talk with her. Nothing formal; more like the banter on the way back along the trail, skirting the brush and the thickets. I said that I loved her place—her sanctuary, I called it. One day when we sat in the Florida room, I said it was enough off the beaten path that I didn't feel completely comfortable with it. Someone else might go there, I said. She promised never to go alone again. All of this was under the condition that I'd be willing to go with her. I promised I would. It was a promise that was not hard to make."

"So you had assurances from Grace that she'd let you go with her."

"Yes, and they were profound, unwavering promises that she made to me, because I think she was sensible enough to perceive my position, and wanted me to know that she understood what was at stake."

"Martha, can you really say you were that sure?" Simon expression was grieved.

"Yes."

His fingers shot to his forehead once again, and he massaged the area around his temples. "And was that the end of it?"

"Not the end of my concern, no. I mean, if Grace showed her private sanctuary to me, she did it willingly. And if she agreed that she had no need or desire to go there without my company, then that could be the end of it. But because these were technically the grounds of Helsey, and there were other residents who could make the same discovery that she had, I took it upon myself to do more, even though I knew Grace might look at it as a betrayal."

Simon waited with the humor of a man who had long crossed his threshold of patience.

"I informed the maintenance staff."

Martha strained to recall the day when she was made privy to Grace's hideaway.

*

She spoke to maintenance, presenting the hazards caused by the lack of a secure fence. George Carney, head of the department, was irked that someone, especially a woman, was telling him how to do his job. George was macho and misogynist to the core, and Martha cringed at the prospect of dealing with him.

He craned his neck to look past her in the hall where they stood, peered beyond, and looked back at the clipboard he held. George was jotting things down. She had to give him credit. Despite his orientation, and obvious annoyance, George agreed that it was an oversight, and was anxious to correct it. Her impression was that they'd get right on it.

Martha turned at the sound of footsteps and nodded to Forrest Greeley. So Greeley's presence was the reason Carney was being cooperative, instantly on his best behavior. Martha thanked him and headed on her way. She was amused in a disgusted sort of way.

*

"Then?"

"I continued to care for Grace, wishing all the while that I could save her. I watched her sliding, caught in the downward spiral, and thought maybe she'd been sent to teach me a lesson. Physicians don't save lives. They only stave the hungry wolves."

Simon stroked his chin. "This is all very philosophical, Martha."

Martha Reed gathered her notepads and her handbag. She stood and smoothed back her hair. She faced Simon Talbot.

"Go to hell," she said, and left.

Chapter 9

SIMON HEAVED A BRIEFCASE full of papers out of his jeep and hauled it into the house. Cindy waited, skulking underneath the kitchen table.

"What have you done?" he asked her, knowing she had something to feel guilty about.

"Cindy, come out here," he commanded. "Cindy." The lanky Labrador crept out toward the foot of her master and whined. Simon caught a glimpse of the cabinet door ajar.

"You couldn't wait for me to come home, so you decided to eat cereal, is that it?" he demanded. The dog whimpered. "Haven't I told you cereal is bad for your teeth?" He grinned, and she wagged a hesitant tail. She had no idea what he'd said, but knew the mood in his voice.

Simon bent to scratch her behind the ear. "I'm not mad at you, Cindy. But you know, Martha is mad at me. She is. Come on over here and I'll tell you about it."

He poured himself a generous swallow of whiskey, retrieved a box of king-sized dog biscuits from the kitchen pantry, and sat with his faithful companion. He'd made Martha furious today. Hadn't seen her like that in years. But it wouldn't hurt Martha to be a little more offended. If she'd adopt a different stance, an offensive posture, her natural instincts would take over. She'd make a better witness and he, in turn, could make a better case.

*

There was a time in medical school when Simon Talbot wore the armor of a sacred knight, and Martha had worshipped him. He was knowledge, and honor, and righteousness. Had her life been charted for a different course, he would be hers, and she, his. Today she had wanted to kill him. How dare he chastise her like that? If he was going to be so damned condescending, she'd just have to give him a written account like the last one. That would serve the same purpose, without the hindrance of hidden agendas: hers, and his alike. She could do without his lofty commentary, and pictured in her mind's eye his expression when he'd said, "This is all very philosophical, Martha."

She took a long hot bath, washed her hair, and used a conditioning pack; the one indulgent thing she'd done for herself lately. The night stretched out for hours ahead. There was time to reflect. More so than in Simon's office. Martha wrapped herself in a thick terrycloth robe, then padded to the kitchen in soft slippers, poured herself a glass of wine, and returned to sit on the living room couch. The computer was faster, but longhand gave more time for the incidents to replay themselves.

She clicked the ballpoint pen, not sure where to begin. Sometimes it was hard to put an exact date on an incident. But the records would date and document themselves. She tried to concentrate on the main events. What Simon was apt to consider important. Damn that man! Martha dove in, and began to write.

I knew that dementia differentiates itself from delirium by its persistence, and the stability of cognitive deficits over time. The distinction between confusional states and dementia was difficult at times. Grace's history had been meticulously reviewed to screen for all drugs that could possibly be responsible for delirium. There were none.

If it were necessary to estimate the level of dementia, at this point, it would be very little. Nothing, save the repetition of questions, gave indication mentally that she was impaired. She had even joked about it.

I answered the questions when I could. Some of the texts suggest ignoring these repetitive inquiries, but I couldn't bring myself to follow this advice. It seemed heartless to just let things go. If they were important enough to ask, I felt I had to reply.

Martha felt a wave of fatigue. It came as a surprise, as she'd planned to stay up most of the night writing. But she could fill in more tomorrow. Then she'd call Simon and try to make amends. Exhaustion made her vulnerable. Maybe she had overreacted. Simon wanted to help. She was convinced that he did.

She went to bed and slept the fitful slumber of dreams. Somewhere in her sleep, the phone jangled loudly. Martha bolted upright, covering both ears with the palms of her hands.

Would he be calling now? She had to think—couldn't talk to him now. There was too much confusion. Her mind was a mass of cobwebs. So much had happened. The ringing persisted. What if it was Simon?

Anxious to answer, yet reluctant to take any chances, Martha let the machine take it. She listened nervously as the voice on the other end made its plea.

"Hello, Martha? It's me. I've been trying to reach you. I'd like to see you...Please, give me a call." And the line went dead. It wasn't Simon.

"I'm just not ready right now," she murmured.

She turned off the ringer on the phone and poured herself another glass of wine

*

Simon bit his tongue. He vowed to keep quiet and not antagonize her. She was walking a tightrope emotionally and didn't need insult added to injury. He was freshly shaven, freshly starched, and well rested. She, on the other hand, looked like she hadn't gotten any sleep. When she walked through the door, he automatically rose and helped her to a chair, thinking about how to say he was sorry.

"Martha…"

"I did a little note-taking last time, but not nearly everything I wanted to cover."

"Are you okay?"

"I'm fine."

"You look like hell."

"I didn't get a lot of sleep."

Simon frowned, arms crossed.

"All right, I didn't get any. But I want to give you all my statements now." She drew three sheets out of a folder, and read what was written on both sides of them. Simon sat for several moments considering her commentary of the night before.

"You talk about the differences between delusion and dementia. Why?"

"Because it becomes an issue. Physically she had the beginnings of apraxia. Hands shaking and, just more instability on her feet."

"Right. And you lectured her on the shoes. But mentally, when was there an issue?"

"On Halloween."

"I see." Simon settled in. "Relive it for me."

"Beg your pardon?"

"Don't just tell it, relive it."

She threw him a doubtful look. "I—all right, I will."

*

The fall season drew nearer, one fallen leaf at a time, and Grace was becoming a veteran at the Institute. As the trees changed for autumn, Helsey also went about preparing for it. Carefully cultivated flowerbeds that were filled with daffodils in the spring, then carnations and violets in summer, now brimmed with mums in red, and orange, and gold. Inside the building, decorative touches of leaves and gilded acorns accented the tables. Horns of plenty brimmed with lacquered gourds and Indian corn. The staff in the cafeteria, the aides, and the nurses thought about the role they'd play on October thirty-first.

Halloween, the ancient holiday that some revered and others ignored. The residents of Helsey had a history of enjoying the thirty-first of October and went full tilt in their costumes and the planning of games and the telling of stories. Especially the telling of stories. Residents and personnel were eligible to compete for best story, which was voted on annually the morning after all entries had been told around the campfire.

George Carney, chief of custodial services, came near to winning every year, and lost by a few votes each and every time, much to his disappointment. This year Carney had promised something special, increasing speculation he would win.

That night was a beauty, with only the hint of a nip in the air. Warm enough for a lightweight sweater, but cool enough to make the stars twinkle and the moon glow yellow as it rose in the sky. People remarked at the wonderful moon, hanging low like the ripest fruit, wanting to be picked. Some residents had family living nearby. Those that could had costumes made, or dressed in peasant-type skirts and wrapped themselves in shawls with warm bandanas covering their heads.

Martha enjoyed Halloween, and filled a bright orange jack-o-lantern with assorted candy, then left it on a sideboard just outside the office. She filled it often, and not coincidentally gained a few pounds each October.

This event was a favorite among the employees and patient community alike. A few nurses had asked if she planned to stay and Martha said she wouldn't miss it, although she never dressed. She saw her last patient at five p.m. and went to the lavatory just off the hallway to wash up. By the time she emerged, the grounds were flooded with children.

Spouses and friends assembled around tables of fragrant cider and freshly baked donuts. Apple pie, apple fritters, walnut bread, banana bread. Martha's mouth watered and she thought fleetingly about those extra four pounds and how tight her suits had become lately. She passed the tables with effort and stopped to watch two men dunking for apples.

A tractor with an attached flatbed rolled up along the driveway, and the maintenance crew, including Mr. Carney helped ready the vehicle for a hayride. Bales of sweet-smelling hay and soft, quilted blankets seated anyone willing, then the tractor took them slowly away, along the paths and through the grounds of Helsey.

A bonfire spit and hissed, then lit the sky, holding vigil. The fire was stoked and trimmed to a neat circle, surrounded by large smooth stones. Remaining bales of hay, also covered with quilts, were lined around the circumference for the storyfest. Martha was impressed at the seamless way one event unfolded into another, knowing all was carefully supervised, and numerous additional employees had been brought in to help, watching out for the residents who blithely sailed through the evening unaware.

Grace was there and she did not dress, although that was open to debate, as Grace seemed always to be in costume. That night, it was a long, white affair that drifted around her ankles as she walked. Martha tried to catch her, but Grace was on the other side of a large crush of people stepping slowly among the guests. She smiled at her new friends, magnanimous to employees and friends alike. An opera-length strand of pearls hung from her neck, and she unconsciously played with them.

At nine p.m., the hayrides ended. The nurses encouraged people to sit around the fire while Carney and his gang brought out marshmallows for toasting. Hot cocoa was passed around, along with hot buttered popcorn in paper sacks. Martha took a seat between two women from the East Wing, and scanned the crowd for the face of Grace Henning. She passed over everyone, then tried a second time to screen closer, until she spotted Grace already sitting, wrapped in gauzy white and waiting.

Carney took a long look around. He waited for the crowd's full attention. When he had it, he began to tell his story.

"This," he said, "is the story of the midnight window. There was once a tiny town called Mythos that doesn't exist anymore. Exactly what became of Mythos and its people is open to debate. Even today, some people say that the town was the victim of a mad phantom who roamed the streets, peering into windows at the stroke of midnight. The phantom lured innocent people from their beds, and scared those people to death…

"Now, Mythos always had a reputation for being a peaceful town. Everybody knew everybody else, and people got together outside of church on Sunday to catch up on the local news."

Carney walked slowly around the circle, pausing now and then to engage his most engrossed listeners—hoping, no doubt, to win their votes.

"Now, one night," Carney said, "at midnight, the peace of the little town was broken. Turns out, one of the town's founding fathers was found dead. Sitting in a chair. Lookin' outa his window.

"Oh, Eli wasn't sick, but he was old. So nobody was surprised when they found him dead. Though the county coroner said he looked like he'd been scared to death. As I say, nobody thought anything of it.

"Eli was buried. And the whole town turned out for the funeral. Afterwards, the residents of Mythos went home, one by one. One man and his wife were overheard sayin' that old Eli was gone, and that was that. The trouble is, that was not that.

"Ya see, a few weeks passed, and the weather turned cold, and the little town settled in for one of a good many long, chilly nights.

"And along early the next morning, another towns-man was found dead. Now, this fella had also been sittin' by a window, with a look on his face like he'd been scared to death. And as the weeks went on, the folks down in Mythos started dying like crazy. And there weren't nobody had the slightest clue what was causin' the deaths, or why the victims had such horrible looks on their faces.

"Finally, the coroner himself was found dead. But he was a smart fella. A man o' science. On the doctor's desk, they found a diary with notes about the mystery. This doctor was makin' one last notation at the very time he died… or was killed. It said, 'I have long been puzzled by the horrific stares on the faces of those poor folk as they come to me in their present condition. What terrible things have they been witness to? There have been only questions, not a single answer. Until last night, at midnight, when a scratching at my window roused me from my sleep. It drew me to the window. There, I witnessed a sight I shall not easily forget.'

"'I peered out to see who might be out at this hour, on a night such as this. And there he was—old Eli himself, looking as if I'd been expecting him. He called to me, wanted me to come outside, but I sank back on my bench, shivering. I drew the blinds in a hurry, lit every candle in the house, and kept from the window until the sun arose. Alas, the day has come and gone, and tonight I am afraid lest Eli pay another visit. I shall beware, and if and when I hear him scratching at my window…'"

Carney moved among his rapt listeners, looking down on them; pausing for emphasis. When he was sure he had them in the palm of his hand, he continued with his story.

"Now that was all the coroner had time to write. Something or someone visited him, all right. They found him dead the next morning. With the frozen, petrified look of all the others.

"Most people cleared out of Mythos after that. The ones that didn't were never heard from again. They say old Eli still roams that part of the country, scratching on windas at midnight, tryin' to find somebody to listen.

"And that's the story of the midnight window. Leave the light on while you sleep…"

A few individuals dared to move, each caught up in Carney's story. And the man's triumphant smile told everyone that he knew for sure that he had won this year's competition. There had been other stories, but Carney's tale had captured the mood of his audience. Tomorrow would tell, and slowly, gradually, people started to fracture away from the locus of the fire.

It was in the afterglow that Grace stepped off into the periphery of the sanitarium's property. Martha wanted to see her, to make idle conversation, and to be sure that Grace enjoyed herself, but she couldn't find her. She wasn't among the ladies of the East Wing—the group she'd helped to dress for *Madama Butterfly*—or the nurses or social workers.

*

Grace was in the dark recesses of the woods when she saw him. At first, no doubt, there were screams falling on deaf ears, as the party was in full swing, and the difference between squeals of delight and those of dismay are easy to hear, but hard to distinguish. And at a certain lull there came a muted cry, and then a louder one, this one clearly for help.

Grace came tumbling out of the brush and onto the scene and Martha stepped forward, catching her by the arm. She was wild-eyed and frenzied. People wondered aloud what was taking place.

"What is it?" Martha turned her around. "Where did you go?"

"I went—" and Grace's eyes drifted over to the thicket. "He—" and she leaned onto Martha's shoulder. "Please. Take me—"

Grace was whisked into a treatment room, arms and legs flailing. She got worse as the minutes passed. Martha tried in vain to get a sense of what had terrified her, then reluctantly sedated her. A healthy dose of Valium would secure the peace of mind Grace needed. Martha drew the medication from the vial, ordering the nurse on duty in the clinic to step aside and let her treat her own patient.

An hour later, Dr. Martha Reed left the joyous event with a pounding headache and the ardent wish that she could indulge in the chemical bliss she knew that Grace enjoyed. There hadn't been time, or the opportunity to really find out what had happened.

Chapter 10

THE NEXT DAY'S SESSION was the most telling of any. In it, Grace admitted that the figment of harlequin still haunted her. She'd had a good night's sleep and had been monitored frequently on orders. Now she sat in Martha Reed's office with a deadpan expression, almost as though none of it had ever occurred.

Martha's own under-eye circles testified to the fact that it had...

"Tell me what you remember about last night," she said to Grace. "If you can."

Grace's empty facial expression conveyed the answer. A frosty scene lay outside the window. So autumn had packed her bags and left, Martha thought bitterly. Just since last night, the season had done her haunting, left the damage, and gone with the memories. Grace had an hallucination, had been sedated, and was now in a blissful state of ignorance. How serene one could be, going through life that way. Martha sank back, defeated. Nothing she could do or say would change anything. She was an irrelevance.

"He's after me, Dr. Reed. He's coming to get me."

"Who is?"

"That…clown…but it isn't funny."

"Which one?"

"He visited me. You know the one! It's the same one I saw in Vera's garden. Everyone thinks I'm crazy."

"You've been asleep for the last several hours. Last night, we gave you medication."

"I know that. Don't you think I know that?" Grace's hostility was thinly veiled.

"You aren't crazy. Your mind isn't functioning well all the time. All parts of it don't work together, as they usually do, that's all."

"I see. So, my brain is a factory. On strike."

Martha let out a sigh. "You may perceive things differently, that's all. Delusions, which are false beliefs to the average person, can be very real to a patient with Alzheimer's."

"Delusions…"

"Hallucinations, on the other hand, are something else."

"What are they?"

"They are events, unreal ones, though you would perceive them as real. I'm afraid it's a little complicated."

"I didn't want to dress," Grace said, with a long breath that added color to her face and stature to her posture.

"Why is that?"

"I knew that if I dressed, he would come. With his purple and green triangles, and his bells."

"Bells." Was it right to pursue a futile line of endeavor?

"The bells on his headpiece, Dr. Reed. Haven't you ever been to Mardi Gras?"

"Yes, I have been there. And I know those colors stand for something, don't they? Prosperity, luck, health— something like that."

"The three bells are at the end of the three points of his hat. They make a tiny sound. It's terrifying…"

Torn between the need to know and the fear of sending Grace over the edge, Martha persisted. "What was the costume made of?"

"Silk," was all she said. Martha wondered for a fleeting instant what hallucinations must feel like. Did they have the same textural sensations as the penetrating feeling of skin being touched?

"And was he wearing a mask?"

"The mask is his face, but you can't read it. So, I guess you could say that the mask is made of skin. It's white. Very white. Chalky and painted. His lips are full and his eyes are painted with tiny little teardrops falling in a line down his cheeks. You feel sorry for him," Grace said, then added, "He never smiles. Poor harlequin."

"And did he speak to you, Grace? Did he say anything?"

"Only with his gestures. Like a mime. Have you ever watched a mime, Dr. Reed?"

Martha told her that she had.

"You long to say what the actor can't get out."

"You want to verbalize for him?"

"Yes." She was definite.

"During the storytelling around the campfire, I saw you. How did you come to be in the woods?"

"I took the tractor ride they had, and left my handbag on the floorboards near the place where I was sitting."

Never mind asking her what she was doing with a handbag she didn't need.

"So, you went back to where the tractor was parked to find it."

"And, I did find my purse. But he was there too."

"The clown."

"The one who's after me." Grace stood and took three steps toward the door. She stopped, and shot a suspicion glance at Martha. "Who am I?" she asked vehemently.

Martha was dumbfounded for want of a reply.

"Just who am I?"

"You're Mrs. Grace Henning."

"I am not! That woman could write her name. I can't write my own name!" She erupted from where she stood, came to the desk and grasped its edges. "You're the doctor! But you can't make me well. You can't make me well!"

Grace was right. And in a moment of absolute clarity, she knew it.

*

Simon raised his hand to still Martha. "What have you got in your personal notebook about the time after that particular meeting? That day when she mentioned the mime?"

"After that date, the medical record might not coincide exactly, because I was keeping a kind of running commentary of my own. I have this entry:

> "Last month's outburst plagues me. I'm finding it hard to come to terms with my own helplessness. The thing plays itself over and over. Apraxia is more pronounced over the last week. Though Grace shuffles when she walks, she keeps on walking. She walks the gardens by day and the halls by night, and never arrives where she is going. She will talk clearly about events that occurred and it's my job to decipher just when they occurred, if indeed they ever did. Grace may be under the impression it was yesterday, but it is sometimes years before.
>
> "And still, her delusions persist. 'The one that's after me,' is how she refers to the man who stalks her.

"There was little I could say to this. I sat, thoughtfully, listening and watching with patient eyes while she collapsed. She rambled across the front lawn for most of the day, listless, apathetic. Pacing back and forth, refusing any offers to do anything else. I watched from my office window, the bundled figure in hat and scarf, and I thought to myself that despite the birds and the trees and the idyllic setting where she walked freely, her prison began with bars squeezing on the inside.

"I worked for two solid weeks to convince Grace she had nothing to worry about; dispelling the notion that she was being stalked."

Martha turned the next few pages of her notebook and sighed. "That's all I have. I told both her and her husband that even the experts don't always agree."

Simon threw down his pad. "Oh, you're right about that. So, you were thinking of what, some kind of persecution complex? As a Jungian Psychiatrist, you would look for signs of a complex. Jung invented the complex."

"True. I suppose I was thinking about ancient archetypes and how they relate to psychotic fantasies."

"And here, you had a case that fit perfectly. Enter the Medieval prototype: harlequin. An ancient buffoon. A harmless relic. These are all wonderful theories. And theories always look good on paper. But in practice?"

"Grace's delusional trigger was the sight of an unidentified male. It could be anyone: a fellow patient's mate or son, a new janitor, or even a new associate psychiatrist. She reacted to all of them with fear and suspicion."

"Did you deny the fantasies?"

"Never. But I didn't play along with them, either. And I always tried to divert her attention."

Simon yearned to console his colleague. "Do you want to take a break?"

"No. I want to go on until it's finished."

"All right."

"November tenth. Grace had a full session on that day. She came in wearing a blue wool dress, and I told her she was looking well.

"And she told me…"

*

"I bought this dress in New York," Grace said. "Bloomingdale's in New York. Have you ever been there?"

"Yes, I've been to Bloomingdale's. I love shopping there when I'm in New York. I guess shopping is one of my real weaknesses. I know you like to shop too."

"And do you go to New York?"

"Not—as often as I'd like to."

"And have you ever been to Bloomingdale's?" Grace repeated.

"Yes," Martha told her again. Her stomach lurched. The repetition of the question was a sign that Grace was getting worse.

"This belt was homemade by my mother's mother's mother. That would make her my...great-grandmother. And it was passed down through generations. The brides in our family wore it as...something blue under wedding gowns."

Martha complimented her on the belt, and the dress, and thought that it was a wonder she managed to dress herself at all. This, despite the fact that her memory was so vivid at times.

"Well, you seem to be in very good spirits," Martha said.

"That's because I'm going out after our session."

"Where are you going?"

"Just out."

*

"I knew better than to press for more. It was an odd day. Not really autumn, not yet winter. The temperature was climbing, but a wayward breeze rustled the branches outside the window. Grace looked out, and it broke our concentration—both mine, and hers—and secretly I think we both wanted to end the session and venture outdoors. As it turns out, Grace did journey out that afternoon. And that was the last I saw of her.

"That night, I went back to the apartment. I felt at peace with my life, and the change of the season, and even my assessment of Grace. The way she was then, happy. Her condition wasn't so very bad. Not then, and I had the feeling it would be a long, long time before she'd reach the stage I'd seen other patients in, where she didn't recognize her surroundings; when her body would forget to function. She had friends. She was going to the ballet. She was dressing half the population at Helsey.

"My sister called and we had a little chat. I asked about our parents. They were well. Sue wanted me to go with her to the movies, but I wanted to stay in. I took a rain check. I spent a while going through my closets and started bringing out my winter clothes. I hate the cold season, but I was resigned to it. It wasn't going to be that bad. I dragged out wool slacks and all the things I hadn't seen since May. There was a full harvest moon that night, and I sat inside with the lights out just looking at it. The calm before the biggest storm of my life.

"At seven, the phone rang, and it was Mr. Greeley from the Institute. He told me that Grace Henning was missing.

"Greeley wanted to know if I had seen her, and when. I told him the details of the afternoon session. It was a scheduled block of time; nothing unusual about my seeing her. She came in, she wasn't distressed, didn't have any upsetting topics to discuss. Greeley said that Grace hadn't shown up for dinner. The staff had been questioned about her usual routine, and they knew nothing. She always came for dinner, and she dressed for dinner, as she'd done over the years before becoming a patient at the center.

"I was stunned at the news. Nothing like this had ever happened to any of our patients. How could it be happening now? And where could she possibly have gone?

"The search party beat a path through the woods. They asked me to help, and I was dreading it, much as I wanted to find her. We called and whistled in case she had gone walking and just gone too far. The security men brought hounds. They gave the dogs articles of Grace's clothing to sniff, and the animals went wild, baying and howling. They tore off through the woods. Security could barely keep up with them. When the dogs rounded the last bend, I saw the gate ajar. And then, of course, I knew.

"We found her at the base of the falls she'd loved so well; face down in the cascading water. I was among the first to arrive amid the noise and confusion. I remember the blue of the water and the blue of her dress. I remember her lifeless body, and not much else. It was my time not to remember."

Martha's voice broke, her eyes brimmed with tears, and she buried her face in her hands.

Chapter 11

SIMON WAS UP and out of his seat. He knelt by Martha's side and put his arm around her. His tone was gentle, reassuring. The words didn't matter, he knew, for the support he might offer. Whatever he could say would be lost, and she would recall only his gestures.

"All right," he said softly, encircling her shoulders with his arm. "Listen. I'm about to break the rules. I know I shouldn't." He helped her up, with few words spoken; consoling, encouraging.

He knew in his heart that they were headed for his cabin, high in the Adirondacks, where only the wind and the trees would bear witness to what happened between them, and only they would judge. He led her down the hallway to the parking lot.

"I'm all right."

"No, you're not. I'm getting you out of here." He guided her into the jeep, grabbing the door handle and wedging his shoulder just inside the door, helping her onto the passenger seat. He looked intently into her face at close range and carefully held her chin between the fingers of his right hand.

"Look at me." She did. Her cheeks were tear-stained as she blinked up at him. "We'll go to my cabin. It isn't far from here. It's quiet. No telephones, no patients."

"I don't know—"

"Trust me." Simon shut her door, went around to the other side, got in, and started the engine. He drove off onto the main artery heading north, never looking over.

"Simon, wait. This is not a good idea."

"Why?"

"I can give you half a dozen reasons why. Starting with reason number one."

"Which is?"

"Which is that you can't have it both ways. You can't review my case and take me up to your house like this, and still be impartial."

"I see. Take the judge out of the courtroom and he becomes a lowlife criminal."

"No."

"What, then?"

"Take the professional man doing a professional service out of the office and put him into a remote cabin with—"

"An attractive female colleague," he prompted.

"Look, I trust you."

"Do you?" Simon asked, eyebrows raised.

"Oh, shut up." He shot her a glance to see whether or not she was serious. Simon chuckled. Now he could relax. And maybe she would too. He'd admit it wasn't the most prudent idea, to take her out of the neutral element of the office. But the winding, sunlit roads leading off the main artery of the Adirondack Northway gave assurance he was doing the right thing. It was necessary, he told himself, to get her to open up. He knew from years of experience that his gut feelings were usually right.

"What else, Martha?"

"I'm tired, Simon."

"I know. That's why we're doing this. But I understand that, as a professional, you can't take this lying down."

"If I were a man, would you have taken me out of the building and driven me up through the mountains to make me feel better?"

Simon balked, still training his eyes on the road. "Do you take me for a fool? I'm not going to indict myself by answering that question."

She was quiet after that, and looked out the window as the vehicle climbed to the rocky plateau where the cabin was seated. Simon slowly got out. He came around to open the door, then held out his hand. When she took it, he held and squeezed it for a moment, before pulling her gently up toward him and out of the car. He looked over his shoulder as Cindy bounded toward them. The dog sensed a special relationship and hovered near, tail wagging, careful not to bark, knowing her master wanted peace.

*

Simon cosseted Martha in his cabin, built a healthy fire, and brought her food. She replied with sheepish thanks, gratefully accepting his kindness. She was fortified by the warmth of a woolen blanket in turquoise and burnt orange. Indian colors with motifs of nature. Martha pulled the thick material up under her chin, watching him move around in the kitchen, mixing some mysterious liquid he claimed would cure her ills.

"Here you are." He handed her a steaming mug. "This will put hair on your chest, if you want it—otherwise, it will just give you courage."

His sense of humor never deserted him, and Martha wanted so to tell him she was sorry for all the miscues of the past handful of years, and that, if circumstances were different, she'd gladly try again. She glanced around the cabin and saw the rustic proof of life in the woodlands. Fishing trophies, photos of campsites, lampshades made of birch bark, and a curious collection of guns in a knotty pine breakfront in a far corner of the room.

"What are those, Simon?"

"Those," he said, "are outlets for male aggression." He grinned. "No, seriously, I have a pretty nice collection of antique guns over there. Original Remingtons, and a number of others. They're just for show," he finished.

"You never take them out of the case?"

"Well, I do carry one in my trunk. I shoot—target practice—up at the Keene Valley Sportsmen's Club, when I get the time. You know I'd be loath to use them in any other way."

"'Never play God.' Wasn't that it?" she asked, quoting the phrase his students attributed to him.

Simon looked quizzical. "Now, what's that all about?"

"You remember. In medical school, they said you were the one most qualified to play God, and the least likely to. Don't you remember that?"

"Don't think so." He pondered, frowning. "What does that mean, exactly?"

"Well, I guess it was pretty obvious how you felt about the various ethical and moral dilemmas. I mean, you were so principled. No matter what medical science unearthed, you'd always argue that we're handmaidens of the Almighty."

"I said all of that?"

"You did." Martha looked over at him fondly. "You were the pillar of all that was good in our profession. Maybe you didn't know it."

"No, I guess not. So, I'm a moral man. There's no harm in that."

"Not in the least."

"There are worse things," he reasoned.

"Much worse." Martha reflected on his reputation for being unable to harm a living thing. And once again, she regretted that she'd hurt him.

"How is it?" He gestured toward the mug she held.

"Oh, wonderful. Hot, and it burns all the way down. Is it supposed to?"

"Yes. It's spiked, do you mind?"

"No."

"I'm sorry. I should have asked."

"It's okay. Really."

"I thought you needed it."

"I have an entertaining suspicion you've done it to incapacitate me."

"Oh, come on."

"In the past, I might have questioned your motives."

"Now, I guess it would be to my credit. At least it would show I hadn't completely gone to seed…"

She struggled not to smile. Finally, they laughed together, knowing that the years apart hadn't changed the bond they felt between them.

They talked for awhile, though Martha knew she was being primed for something more exacting. Somehow she didn't mind. Finally he looked resolutely down at his own mug and said, "You know, I didn't bring you here only for the company."

"I know you have to go on with the investigation. And, whether you do it here, or at your office, doesn't matter to me."

"Okay," he nodded. This was what he must have wanted: permission to go on. "We just have to get it over, Martha." It looked as if it pained him to say it, and he downed a hefty tumbler of bourbon and placed the glass on the coffee table. Martha decided it had been to her advantage that they ended up here. He had a right to know everything.

"Simon, I can't undo what's happened in the past."

"I know."

There are a lot of things that, maybe I misjudged or acted foolishly on, but I did what I was driven to do at the time."

"That goes without saying." He moved a few inches closer and frowned. "Look, you need to be frank with me. Can you do that?"

Could she?

"I want you to read what you'd written, to go into the permanent record," he said.

"It isn't what's in the record, Simon. It's what isn't there."

Martha had approved of coming here, of being caught defenseless in his home base, and now she knew she'd have to play by his rules. No matter how disturbing, the facts had to surface. It was better, she reasoned, for her to be the one to disclose the events, than anyone else. She got up and walked to a window seat above the pine forest, and found her notebook. She pulled it open, and found the spot.

"Here it is," she said.

He indicated the sofa where he sat. He wanted her to sit next to him. She hesitated, then crossed the room and settled on the sofa.

"I kept a small notebook of my own, which had things in it I didn't want to share…things that were inappropriate to share in the record."

"All right."

"Unofficial things."

He nodded. She read.

"Grief. An inevitable response to loss. Read in the shadowy features of the spouse that's left behind. To grieve, to mourn, to pick up the pieces. Or try to fit them back into the shattered frame of life. I had seen that look in the eyes of John Henning many times, and when he wrote to me it was the image of that shadowy face that stayed with me.

"His letter was postmarked months after the accident. Most of it could easily be some generic excerpt from a hundred letters of family members, stashed in the files of my colleagues. But there was one section of it that struck me, and it added to the rhyme in my head that played itself over and over, bubbling just beneath the surface…"

Martha hesitated. Simon wore the look of a man about to be handed a death sentence.

*

The envelope sat, unassuming, in a pile of bills mailed to her home. She ripped it open, puzzled, gratified. John Henning—after so many months. How had he managed and what was he doing now? White laid stationery. Heavy, textured. Yes, this was a Henning standard.

He began by saying that he'd wanted to write sooner; that he appreciated the care and attention that Martha had taken of his wife over the months. "I've loved Grace," he said, "the person that she was, and I never understood the urgency—the few remaining moments that were left to me to make my peace with her. This thing had crept into our lives and taken her from me. And I never knew that she was leaving."

Martha crumpled the paper in her hands, dropping down into a chair. All the pain came charging back. She hadn't gotten over Grace, her lovely smile, and her sense of humor. This wasn't the way it was supposed to be. She was a doctor. That meant detachment and objectivity. She had never had that when it came to Grace. A stinging tear became two, until her eyes swelled with dollops of saltwater welling up, surging out, and pelting the crumpled, costly paper. She rallied to unfold the dampened material, thinking it was a shame to ruin it. The letter went on and the rest was essentially insignificant. He would make an appointment to see her.

Martha held the used and ragged letter in her hand, reviewing it, before he came. It had been read until she knew it by heart, but the feel of what had been fine paper gave her a sense of substance. She had an awful, chilling vision of Grace's exquisite face rotting in her grave, and shook it off. The textbooks had told her that the one who was left behind would be faced with the prospect of starting a new life, and that "the when" and "the how" was a sensitive, cloudy issue. There was no distinct schedule to be followed. What was right for one spouse was unthinkable for another. Some people went on for years, enshrining the life they'd shared with their mates. Others went right out, meeting new people without pause. The journals said that counseling for the remaining spouse was essential. But what the textbooks never taught was how to deal with what followed.

*

At four thirty p.m., she let her secretary go. Julie Smith had an appointment at five, and Martha saw no reason to have her stay. She spent the time ambling around the office, to look distractedly out the window, and to wonder how she could possibly console John Henning.

He entered quietly, came through the reception area, paused at her door, and knocked lightly, clearing his throat. "Hello."

Martha turned. "There you are… Please, come in."

Charcoal gray silk shirt, open collar. Black linen slacks, starched and pressed. These were the things that registered.

"It's nice to see you," she said. She wondered if he'd wrinkle when he sat. Somehow she didn't think he would. "Would you like to have a seat?" And then when he did, she asked, "How have you been?" It sounded inadequate even to her.

"All right. I suppose." He looked around, surveying the room. "You've made some changes."

"Oh, have I? No, it's the cleaning woman. She changes things. Switches the pictures. She's afraid I might get bored."

"And do you?"

"Well, no. My work keeps me occupied so much of the time… I've been meaning to get in touch with you. I wanted to express my sympathy."

"And I wanted to thank you. Sincerely, thank you very much indeed."

"It's never easy. I've had patients before with the same illness that Grace had. Of course, she was younger than most."

"Yes. It was a terrible waste."

"I wish I'd been able to do more. I was at the funeral."

"Yes. I saw you there."

"You saw me?"

He nodded. "I knew that you came. And it means a lot because I know your time is at a premium. I had wanted to get in touch with you as well, but…it might have been unseemly. To have contacted you sooner."

The statement caught her off guard. She tried to reconcile it during the drifting conversation that followed. Surely he must have known that she was available to counsel the spouse of a former patient.

"I've been hard at work on the toll road case," he went on. "You may have read about it in the papers."

"You alone, or your associates?"

"I like to work my cases alone. Being the head of the firm, I can pick and choose. It has its disadvantages, but I have only myself to blame—or to congratulate."

Martha strained to recall what she'd read about the case. "Oh, now I know the one. Are you representing the State or—"

"Not the State, good God, no. There'd be no challenge in that. My client is an individual."

"You've been putting in long hours," she remarked.

"Very, very long hours. I've fairly buried myself in my work. But then, I suppose that's normal."

"It's what most people do. It helps the healing process."

"I've been going through her clothes…" He trailed off, clearly uncomfortable.

She sensed his discomfort, and interrupted, "Excuse me—Mr. Henning—would you like something to drink? Hot coffee or a cup of tea? How inhospitable I am—I never even thought to ask."

"No, thank you." Henning shifted in his seat, looked closely at her, then got up and stepped toward the bookcase. His back still to her, he asked, "Would you mind calling me John?"

He turned to face her, looked her dead on and, without waiting, immobilized her with his appeal. "Would you be available to have dinner with me? The Polo Club puts on a tantalizing meal, with music and dancing."

She stood, baffled and unprepared. She'd been expecting—what had she expected? Blood drained, then filled her face by turns, and she was both flattered and stunned by his interest.

"You see, my life is so unresolved," he said. "I can't seem to go forward. I just wanted to talk, that's all."

"I know." She didn't. Didn't know, didn't comprehend.

"I could call you," he offered, "in a few days, so you could check your schedule."

"All right," she heard herself say, remembering nothing of what transpired from that moment until he left.

She had no plans, but couldn't bring herself to give him a definite answer.

She needed to get home. She had to share this with someone who would be able to make some sense of it. She certainly couldn't. She and Mother were close, but Martha knew better than to relate the details to her. Mother would somehow turn it into a lecture. Martha didn't need instruction. She needed a friend.

Martha took the long way home. She drove along one long stretch of county road past cow pastures and riding stables. This was her safe route, the one to cruise along when her mind needed to wander. When she reached the apartment, she dropped her coat and briefcase just inside the door, flicked on the light, and grabbed the phone. She called Susan and asked her to come over. Right away.

*

"What's really going on here, sis?"

Martha halted, tray in hand. "I just told you. He came in to the office. I got his letter."

"What was in the letter?"

"Just the usual." Martha set a cheese board filled with Brie and crackers within arm's reach of her sister. She returned to the kitchenette for another tray, this one bearing a teapot and cups.

"No beer to go with these crackers?" Susan stuffed her mouth as she spoke.

"Do you want beer?" Martha hadn't given a thought to that. Susan was a big fan of cheese and crackers, and she always drank beer with it. "Say no more. Sorry. I wasn't thinking. But I won't be able to join you. I need a clear head. Have a lot to think about."

"What did you mean, the letter was just the usual?" Susan asked. "That means, just a thank you note for being her physician."

"Yes, pretty much that. And I was only surprised that he hadn't sent it sooner. I wasn't expecting it, you understand; I just thought maybe he would have done it by now, if at all."

"So he comes in to see you and the gist of it is what? 'Thanks for all you've done, can we go out and talk more?' Or 'Thanks—and are you free to go out?'"

"I don't know what he meant. I think he's just mourning her, and these people in this situation project a sort of attachment to their spouse's physician somehow."

"Makes sense," Susan said between gulps from the frosty mug. "Martha, this is great beer. Sure you don't want any?"

"No."

"I don't get it, Martha. What's the big deal? He's depressed and wants to talk to you about it. Maybe he doesn't want to become a psychiatric patient himself. You know it still does carry a stigma for a lot of people."

"And this a way of talking about it, in a neutral setting." Martha was beginning to see Susan's line of thinking. The truth was that she was disturbed by the prospect of seeing him socially, even once.

"Just because you're not going to be sitting there with your spectacles on, taking notes, doesn't mean you can't give the man good advice. Besides, you might get a nice dinner out of it. I hear some of those clubs are really posh."

"I don't care about that, Sue."

Susan shook her head. "What a waste. Maybe I can go in your place... Martha, you're all worked up over nothing. You're overreacting. The man made a normal request. It's simple. If you dated more, you'd be familiar with the practice."

"All right, I get the point. But you see, this is not about dating. This is about a serious, tragic thing that happened to this man, and I'm just not at my best when I'm out of the office."

"He doesn't want a professional, Martha. He just wants somebody to listen."

"Well, maybe you're right." She felt her reserve slipping.

"Did he come on strong or anything?"

"No, no."

"Make a pass at you in the office? You said Julie was gone already. You were alone with him, right?"

"We were all alone." Susan made a good point. It was a simple, basic request. And it was courteous and understated like everything he did. Why should she be so opposed? A respectable six months had elapsed since Grace's passing.

"Just stop beating yourself over the head with it, sis," Susan said. "Go with him. Have dinner and tell him you're sorry about his wife. Then, let him do the rest of the talking. Isn't that what you people do: say a few things, ask a couple of open-ended questions—and let the person dig themselves in deeper and deeper? You nod your head and say, 'Um hmm, Yes.' That's it, then you send an enormous bill a couple of weeks later."

"That's awfully kind of you, Susan."

"Forget about that. What are you wearing?"

"Wearing!"

"Well, you've gotta wear something. You can't go looking like a slob, and this is one time that white coat won't pass muster. You need a nice dress, an ensemble, or a—how about a black dress? That goes anywhere. I've got one. You're only a half size smaller than me, and I bet this one I have in mind would look gorgeous on you."

"I don't know. Chances are I'm not going anyway."

"You're a fool if you don't go. I'd go regardless. It's a place you've never been. You'll meet all kinds of interesting people. You'll feel better because you gave him the chance to talk to somebody about his wife. Look, Martha. Just borrow the dress. I'll drop it by tomorrow."

*

Two days later, Martha sat in the study of the apartment, trying to ignore the phone. She was still in a quandary. She'd rehearsed all contingencies either way. First she'd planned to say no, that her schedule was just too full. But he would probably offer to wait, even if it meant they would plan far into the future.

In the next scenario, she would go with him, but only once, and act as if she wanted nothing more than to be his friend. She had considered Grace a friend. But a voice insisted that nothing good could come of this. The voice said, tell him no.

When the call did come, Martha's hands shook as she reached for the phone, even though she anticipated his call.

"Hello." *What does he want from me?*

"Oh, hello, Martha."

He was tentative when he asked, "Is it all right? Am I catching you at a bad time?"

His voice was soft, almost pacific, and she could picture him sitting at his own desk, cradling the receiver. Martha closed her eyes to conjure the image of John Henning's polished features, the soulful blue eyes—and shook her head to clear it. She felt so out of her depth in this— no way to prepare—and she disliked the loss of control. It was a taste in her mouth, acrid and annoying.

"How have you been?" she forced out.

"Well, I've been okay. Just out of sorts lately, you know?"

A stab of regret needled at her, and then, a wave of guilt.

"I know. It must be very hard." She wanted to make small talk, wanted to ask him how his case was getting along, and a dozen other things she would have been able to had it not been for the uneasy circumstances.

"I won't keep you," he was saying. "I just wanted to see if you'd checked to see if you might be free to have dinner with me. At the club. I just thought we could talk." He faltered, and she dove in to help him recover. Yes, here was a man in grief, shattered and irreconcilable. She could hear it in his voice. In the span of a few seconds he'd gone from serene to unsure.

"I'd like that," she said.

They agreed to meet the following evening, and he offered to come by for her at the Institute. She'd be working late, with two new admissions to deal with and plenty of paperwork to accompany them.

Stilling doubts, she made the arrangements and ended the phone call quickly, politely. It was easy to consider only her own feelings, but what about him? Hadn't he suffered?

Chapter 12

THERE WAS A TIME when Martha wouldn't dream of slipping into the little black sheath that Susan had lent her. She thought about the emotional quality black inspired. Peculiar, for her, it was the stuff of mourning clothes. But for the majority of people it was also the height of sophistication, and something darker too. *Seductive* came to mind. It bothered her that it might be seen as something other than a casual meeting of friends bound by a common tragedy. She was loathe to send the wrong message, especially when her choice of dress was one of the few things she'd be able to influence.

She wore little jewelry. Deep chestnut locks fell about her shoulders. It was amazing how she'd had to plan so purposefully to achieve a simple affect.

John was prompt, punctual to the nth degree, and when he came in the office, a smile lit his handsome features, and she almost forgot that they were both players with time left on their contracts. Neither of them must step out of character.

John glanced briefly, admiringly, as he stepped into the room. "Martha. You look lovely."

The words flowed naturally from his lips. Automatically. How many times had he said those words, and to how many women?

She allowed herself to be led down the walk to the curbside. John opened the door to a midnight-blue Mercedes, and paused to look at her squarely. "What are you laughing at?" he wanted to know.

"Nothing."

"Come on."

"I don't know. Somehow, I was—thinking about your car."

"What's wrong with my car?"

"Nothing, but I might have guessed you'd be driving something like this."

She slipped into her seat. The door closed with a solid thud. John came around and slid in beside her. He pivoted toward her. "Am I so very predictable?"

She adjusted her seatbelt and, for some counterfeit purpose, foraged in her handbag. She thought wryly that the term *clutch purse* had real meaning for women on dates. It was nonsense, ridiculous. She was not a teenager, and this was not a date.

The car held the road like an upper moving layer of it, and Martha nestled back, allowing herself to sink into the luxury that was the world of John Henning. It was the feel of leather beneath her thighs, and the heady smell of his aftershave. John's Mercedes swept past trees that ended in a blur, and she closed her eyes. She didn't mind. So many months of endless struggle, fighting a losing battle with Grace. Pangs of remorse shot through her.

The car turned onto a cobblestone drive and a sign announced, MOHAWK CLUB. Members Only. High, rising peaks of a Tudor mansion rose above the treetops, partly hidden behind massive pines. Heavy boughs lay in soft folds, muffling the sounds around them, making the structure seem surreal. Martha leaned forward for a better view.

"Goodness," she muttered.

He looked over, taking his eyes from the driveway for a second. "What's the matter?"

"It's just that I feel like a fish out of water."

"What do you mean?"

"You belong to all of this."

"You're joking." He chuckled, and this time, his eyes glittered. "And you don't?"

"I can't imagine…" She trailed off.

John slid out of his seat, came around, and leaned over her until they came face to face. "Come in, Martha. The water's fine."

He held his arm out and led her to the towering structure enveloped in the hardwoods. Once inside, they took their places milling among the smart set sampling hors d'oeuvres. She imagined a hush falling over the room as they entered, but if his club-mates thought it odd that they were together, they gave no indication.

She caught snatches of nearby conversation.

"The proceeds from the ball go to the university fund for grant scholarships for indigent students," said one elderly man to another.

A trio stood near. "—Professor Brown," Martha heard a woman opine, "he's the best-looking faculty member. Every underclassman's dream."

A second concurred, "Brown is my favorite too."

"Swoon if you will," the third told them, "but remember, if you decide to take courses with him, he's a very hard marker."

"You're saying that because you can't finish your play," the first woman speculated.

So this was the scuttlebutt within the walls of the Mohawk Club. It was what Martha expected. Fundraising and social issues, with a little gossip thrown in.

She stood ensconced in the circle of John's admiring friends. John himself was quiet-spoken, yet commanded the attention of everyone around. Still, he wasn't her type, and never could be under the circumstances.

She let her mind wander enjoying the mental picture of it all, coming to, moments later to discover John's attendant look.

"I'm sorry. I was just daydreaming."

"Well, stop daydreaming. There are people I'd like you to meet." He went about the room, introducing her, exchanging pleasantries, and artfully dodging topics that wouldn't include her—wanting, it seemed, for her to feel at home.

A low voice intruded gently as a white-gloved steward said something to John. The man ushered them to an outdoor terrace with small tables set for two, draped in white linen and topped with matching candles. All was white but the shadows. And the mood and flavor shifted with the flickering flames.

"Everything all right?" He arched one brow, studying her.

"Oh, it's lovely!"

"Generally we wouldn't be sitting here for another month or two. Seasonally we just don't get these temperatures this soon." Martha didn't seem to hear him. She was too busy taking in the ambience of the club.

"Would you like to dance?" John stood as though he expected she would say yes.

"I haven't danced in a long time."

"Then it's been far too long. Come on."

I'm not ready for this, she told herself. I wasn't planning on this. Thoughts and questions raced through her mind. They stepped into the crowd. Lightheaded, Martha began to perspire. John Henning watched, eyes penetrating, blue. Blond hair gleamed like flowing honey touching his white collar. He smelled of heady aftershave, and she drew the scent in deeply, felt the firm hand on her lower back, guiding her, and silently she willed for the moment to never end. They talked as they danced, in soft tones, as their bodies molded into one swaying shape, little movement, head to head. John's lips brushed her ear, and the conversation had an intimacy to it.

John told her about his comrades who were there; some dancing, some watching the two of them as they danced. Martha guessed from what he told her that he was on good terms with most of them; a godfather to one man's son, college fraternity brother to another, and fellow member of the bar association for several of the others. It seemed the room was full of attorneys.

"No doctors in this club?" she asked playfully.

"We let only pretty female ones in, Martha."

"I hope I pass the test," she joked.

"You pass, all right." He brought her slightly closer and breathed into her ear, "With flying colors."

Martha let the tension she'd been feeling flow down and away. She hadn't planned to enjoy this, but she was.

When it ended, she felt in a daze. John led her to the outskirts of the room, off to an alcove.

"That was nice." He beamed down at her. "It's odd to see you in a different setting. Away from the clinic." John paused to greet two club members who knew him. "Peter." He nodded to a tall stocky man. The other sent a fleeting, appreciative look her way, and Martha had a brief impression that she must be passing inspection.

John asked if she'd drink champagne, and they sat over steamed mussels and lobster bisque. She contemplated him here, in his element, and wistfully imagined they'd met otherwise. He would be the perfect escort, lover or husband, and she pictured him with Grace. What did the two of them talk about? And was he comparing her now? She resolved to channel the tone of this evening, so that they could remain friends. She knew that for her, he could never be anything else. With resignation, she let it all sink in.

"How is your practice?" he wanted to know.

"Fine. How is yours? You mentioned your office is in the downtown district. I don't get to that part of town often, but it's charming the way they've kept the historic character of it."

"Mmm, the mayor is very particular about the zoning and that sort of thing. Variances are hard to get. Not that I've applied for one recently."

John cocked his head to one side and lowered his voice. "Look, Martha. What's gone before is something that neither of us can change."

"Listen, John—I just don't want to talk about it now—if you don't mind. This thing has been going on in one small way or another in all the months since Grace died."

"Typical of legal matters. They always tie people up far longer than they have to."

"Sounds funny, coming from an attorney."

"Well... But how can you say that you won't discuss it? You're a psychiatrist. You people talk about everything, don't you?"

"And I have a duty and responsibility toward my patients."

"I am not your patient, Martha."

"No. Of course not."

"Then correct me if I'm wrong. I thought this was a social occasion. Let's do both of us a favor and not put any preconceived notions on tonight. Please. You know, it's been so very long since I've been able to be with anyone."

"It's only been a little while since she—"

He cut her off. "Since my wife died. But it's been a lot longer since we'd been together."

She was offended by that, and she wanted to say so. True, some people found solace in the arms of someone else, though their spouses were still alive. As a professional, she recognized it as just one of many issues. But here, tonight, it seemed somehow unthinkable—out of the question. Martha had been ambivalent in the past; now she knew what her advice would be in the future, to the spouse that was left behind.

Chapter 13

SIMON SAT, RATIONAL and calculating, weighing yet disbelieving, as Martha described the tenuous atmosphere as she and John Henning left the Mohawk Club.

*

It was about midnight. Most other guests and members had drifted off and left before them. Martha had gone with John down to the dock below the granite terrace to look at the sailboats moored there. John knew two or three people who owned the boats, and introduced Martha to them. They were invited to climb aboard one of the larger ones, more like a houseboat than a sailboat, and the owner served them trays of salmon and capers with whole wheat toast points, just out of the oven. The gentleman insisted his wife didn't generally know how to cook, but served up a delicious array of fine appetizers.

After yet another glass of champagne, Martha noticed that her perceptions of things had gone blurry, and she wondered how John had fared. But he was sober. More than sober, somehow. He moved with the same careful precision he always had. Said the same polite things, and glided easily from one phase to another. Martha nodded toward the door, begging him with her eyes to take her home, and he complied, making their exit as smooth as their entrance had been.

For the first time that she could remember, she didn't know how to proceed. Things were different now. She wasn't the authority figure. In fact, she knew that John Henning had the upper hand. From the first turn out of the club, she worried like a schoolgirl about what would happen next. She berated herself for it, but to no avail. She still speculated how to end the night when they pulled up in front of the condo.

John dutifully held the door for her, smiled graciously, and took her arm to meander up the brick walkway. The porch was a wide, flat concrete slab, with round white columns and an overhang. They came to a halt under the small canopy just as a rumble of thunder sounded overhead. Martha looked up.

"Looks like a storm brewing," he said, never taking his eyes from her.

"I have early morning rounds at the hospital."

"I understand."

"Otherwise I'd invite you in." More thunder, and she fished nervously in her purse for her keys. As she pulled them out, he deftly reached over and took them from her.

"Allow me." John inserted the key, turning it easily. "You're all right?"

"Yes."

"Haven't had too much to drink."

"No."

"Liar." He winked.

"It was wonderful—very nice. I don't want you to think that I didn't enjoy it."

John's eyes glistened, two deep pools in the moonlight. He edged closer. "May I kiss you goodnight?"

She took a step back.

"Does it have to be so awkward between us?" he asked.

"No, I'm sorry."

"I don't want it to be," he said casually.

She smiled weakly. "Neither do I. I'm usually not so unsure of myself."

"Well, I'm not in the least unsure." He reached for her, pulling her in, until a dense and muscled thigh came between her own, and his hands buried in her hair, pulling it back and up from her face. He looked directly at her lips and covered them with his own, then drew a long and lingering kiss, followed by another. Finally,

Martha pulled back a few inches. She was suffocated by him. Overwhelmed.

"I have to go."

He held her close a fraction longer, then stepped back. "Well then, you mustn't dally."

Thunder overhead. They both looked up, and Martha inched toward the door. "Once it starts coming down, the roads will be slick," she warned.

"Yes, I suppose."

She pushed open the door, and turned to him. "Be careful. And, thank you."

She couldn't quite look at him, but stepped over the threshold and entered the house. The solid door closed behind her like a punctuation. She leaned against it, eyes shut, and ran a shaking hand through her hair.

*

Outside John Henning stood still in the spot where he'd kissed her, though the rain sprayed down all around him. "Good night, Martha," he whispered.

*

"So you wrestled with your conscience, is that it?" Simon got up from the sofa and walked to the casement window, cranking it open, needing the air and the space. He spun around to face her. His disapproval was palpable. So was his contempt.

She wondered what would she do if he found against her. She tried to picture a life without that coveted degree;

no license to practice medicine. Had there been any other dream since she was a child? And how, she wondered, do you reconstruct a lifelong dream? Would she cast about, asking old colleagues for references, or just let herself decline as a recluse holed up in that desolate condo she called home? All of her eggs, all of them were in one basket. How would she survive?

His eyes had never left her face. "Is nothing sacred, Martha?"

She knew she faced the loss of her best and only ally. And she couldn't bear the thought of losing him. And there was something more. Martha knew when he looked at her that way, it was somehow more important for Simon to respect her, than it was to keep her precious license.

"He sought me out. I suppose, he had been alone for so long—even before Grace was found dead. She wasn't able to be a companion to him."

Simon turned away. "Or a lover. So you had to do it for her?" His voice rose.

Martha jumped up and came to within a few feet of him. "I beg your pardon?" There was a strength she received, from the personal injustice.

"Have the guts to be honest with me, and with yourself. Just how did you really feel about John Henning?"

"I felt nothing."

"When did you begin to feel attracted to him—early on?"

"No."

"At about the time you realized Grace couldn't service him anymore?"

"No." Martha took a furious step forward. "What is it about men, anyway, Simon? It all boils down to sex for you."

"The knives are out at the palace, I see. You can put away all of those weapons. Don't forget, I'm the one who taught you everything you know."

He went back to the window, brooding and morose.

"So tell me, how was it between you?" he asked.

Martha drifted off, touching her lips, reliving Henning's kiss. For a ten-second eternity she was off, then she came jerking back to the present.

"Decide to step in and provide what was missing?" he demanded.

She heard the jealousy dripping in his voice. "Oh shut up, Simon, and listen to me. I loved that woman and I wanted desperately to help her. I actually thought I could."

"Alzheimer's disease is incurable."

"But I was there for her. I wanted to be. I didn't plan for any of what happened. I swear to God I never did anything unethical!"

"Never gave him signs?"

"Never."

"Just a little question mark, perhaps?"

"No, Simon. You've got it all wrong. I was shocked when he contacted me. It was something I couldn't possibly foresee. I was unprepared and confused and I spent the next two weeks avoiding his phone calls, or making excuses about being too busy to see him."

He buried his head in his hands, obviously weary. Spent. He spoke quietly, "What else haven't you told me?"

"Nothing. I swear it."

"What about the fence?"

"What—"

"The fence at Helsey. After she brought you there, you told them to fix the opening."

"Yes, I did. And they fixed it, but, I don't know. Somehow she—"

"Buck up, Martha, you don't seem too sure. If this case is about negligence, this point is crucial. The fact is that she was an Alzheimer's patient who may have wandered off to that spot. Your role as caretaker dictated you take action to prevent her from wandering there again."

"And I did take action."

"You say she knew the place."

"Oh, she knew it."

"Knew how to get there."

"Yes. I told you."

"Determined that she would take you there—that blows the theory…"

"What theory?"

"Because a man owns a cattle farm does not mean he had beef for dinner. Necessarily."

"What are you talking about?"

"She was an Alzheimer's patient, so she might have been expected to wander. But that doesn't mean that she did wander. The falls were her destination. She went there—into the woods—with intention."

"She promised me she wouldn't go there again, alone. But she forgot. She did forget things, Simon, and that is a sign of the disease."

"She forgot. Maybe."

Chapter 14

THE RIDE BACK to Simon's office was uncomfortable. Neither of them talked. He spoke only to tell her he would wait while she started her car and drove out of the deserted parking lot.

Martha headed home, mind numbed, relieved to be out of his jeep. Her car knew the way; her hands steered, her foot used the brake mechanically. The active part of her brain was working on something far more important. How had she gotten into this? How was she going to ever get out?

She knew Simon would be angry about John. But that was a separate issue. She had told him the truth when she said she had felt nothing. The fact was, she was feeling more for Simon lately. Some of the old sentiment was back. Maybe it had never left. What went wrong between them?

My own fault, she reasoned. She hadn't given him the time of day, wouldn't take time off from her quest to be a great doctor, to be a normal woman with average needs. She never wanted to be average. That, in essence, was the problem. There were instances when she could have picked up on his clues, openings when even a smile or a kind word, some inkling of interest, would have paved the way. But she had been wary of him and other men who would waylay her from the quest. Her journey, her calling. How insolent. How presumptuous. What did she possibly hope to accomplish? A cure for insanity in its endless forms? She laughed aloud. She couldn't so much as cure her own mental anguish, let alone that of mankind.

And for Simon's part, he sat by patiently waiting, and probably hoping she'd notice how much he cared. Of course, she knew. But she just didn't have time. Too late now, surely. He'd never give her a second chance. Would he?

*

Simon faced the bathroom mirror, peering at his bristled features. He slathered shaving cream over his face, and let out a moan of pleasure at the sensation of the hot foam. Clouds of steam rose as hot water gushed from the faucet.

He hadn't stopped thinking about Martha from the moment he'd dropped her off at her car. The frustration and resentment gained strength overnight. What bothered him was that Martha dishonored Grace's memory, and that was the worst that could be said. But his own resentment outshone all else.

He felt cheated, that a man like Henning could steal Martha out from under him. Henning was smoothness and charm incarnate, that was true, but couldn't she see beyond the polish? Hadn't she gone for the common hero, been the champion of the underdog in the past? Could Martha have changed that much in the last few years?

It alarmed him to admit, even to himself, that he had seen the case as an opportunity to get close to her again. Martha's vindication had never concerned him; he was sure about her abilities and her compassion. But why had she gone for Henning, if she did? She denied it, of course. She'd have to. Especially to him.

Did she know what he felt? Could she possibly imagine that it took every ounce of restraint he had not to jump over his desk and grab and kiss her and squeeze the heck out of her. Sometimes when he woke at night, her dark hair covered him and she stared across the pillow at him, green eyes seeing through to his soul. And then he'd realize it was all a dream. What did goddamn John Henning have that he didn't?

Simon commanded himself to the task. An unbiased clinician could reasonably assess the newest events; a lovesick suitor could not. He'd go over it one more time.

Initially the diagnosis was accurate. And Grace's disease was characterized by, what? Forgetfulness, disorientation, delusional thinking, hallucinations. Sometimes regression into childish behaviors. Instinct told him the key lay in what they somehow already knew.

After her admission to Helsey, Grace had begun to change physically, and she'd lost certain word associations. Martha said she also walked aimlessly up and down the halls. But that meant boredom. "Wandering" could be a misnomer. She still had rational, logical thinking abilities left largely intact, and was somewhat a creature of habit. The regulated scheduling of her life under the careful supervision at the Institute had contributed to that. He saw this as something positive, like a backbone she could lean and depend on.

He had a good hour's drive ahead of him to meet Henry at the lake. He dressed in a hurry, still preoccupied. Despite the small amount of sleep, and his major preoccupation with Martha and her case, he'd make his meeting with his old college friend.

The sturdy jeep pulled onto the smooth ribbon of road into traffic. He thought of Henry, always studying the law. Henry had a quick tongue and a ready sense of humor. He could always deal with the bad jokes that followed his pursuit of a law degree. The highway narrowed, but the jeep was surefooted. He cruised at a comfortable speed. His mind went back to Martha. And Grace.

*

"Dr. Talbot?" The barmaid at the lodge greeted Simon with a basket of cashews and a Rusty Nail. "Mr. Jameson said you'd be ready for this when you came. He's out on the porch, doctor. I'll take you there." Simon followed her, drink in hand.

She passed through a smallish doorway of roughhewn birch beams and opened the way to a staggering outlook. A wraparound porch traveled the length of the lodge. There were dark green pieces of wood furniture, and plenty of cushions. Henry leaned against the knotty pine railing.

"Simon, you made it!" Henry turned, smiling broadly, and the two exchanged strong and healthy handshakes.

"Sit down, Simon. Take a look at Lake Placid."

"Rightly named. So, this is how you spend your time, Henry."

"You've never been here? They had the Winter Olympics here, remember? Did you meet Alice?"

"Alice? Oh, the nice lady who made my drink."

"Now, you're catching on. I want you to tell me all about the world of modern shrinkology. Can you do that in, say, two and a half hours?"

Simon took a long drink from his glass. "I don't know if you remember, Henry, but in college I laid you out flat a couple of times. You came at me with some nasty little argument about lawyers—why the world needs twice as many lawyers and half the number of doctors. Something like that."

"Right. I remember."

"Well, I can still take you, so watch it." Simon grinned.

Henry made sure Simon's glass was never empty. It hadn't gone unnoticed. Simon drank the second Rusty Nail, then asked his friend point-blank, "Is this going to be one of those binge-drinking sessions we were both so good at in college, Henry? Because if it is, you'd better tell me and I'll see if they've got a room for me to crash in for the night."

"It's all taken care of. We can go in for dinner, then close the bar. We've got reservations for the night. They are holding two rooms for us."

"Why didn't you tell me?"

"Well, for one, I was afraid you'd say no. You doctors are always on call or some other nonsense. My second, self-seeking reason, is that we haven't had one of those binge drinking things in ten or fifteen years."

"Well, I don't know about you, Henry, but my liver isn't as young as it used to be. College men can handle it. I'm not sure you and I can."

Henry chuckled and brought out a pipe, filling it with tobacco. "I wanted the time to discuss this predicament you're in, Simon. Man to man."

"My predicament. Which one is that?"

"Your love life."

"Oh, God. Spare me."

Henry lit the pipe with a smile. He clearly had no intention of sparing Simon. He took an extended drag and exhaled the pungent smoke, letting Simon stew for a minute. "Don't tell me there's no predicament. There is. If you can't see it, then all I can say is, it's a good thing I dragged you up here."

Simon crossed and uncrossed his legs. He took another sip of his drink, and looked out over the water, exasperated. "Where is this coming from?"

"The last I knew, you were midway through the exploratory stages of this inquest."

Simon raised a hand. "No, no, wait. That hasn't got anything to do with—"

"Your love life? Not true. They're interrelated. One and the same. You have the official progression of events, and then you have the unofficial—"

"Skip it, Henry. I'm not in the mood."

"My word, you're an ugly drunk."

Simon was up and out of his seat, angry in spite of himself. He turned his back on Henry, unable to look him in the face. Henry's hand was on his shoulder, "Hey, hey. Sorry. None of my business."

"It's not that." Simon stared long and hard at the closest thing for a confidant he had in the world. He let out a heavy sigh. "Do I have to tell you all my secrets?"

Henry led his friend back to a wooden chair. "Only the ones I ask about."

*

They talked over dinner in the lodge's dining room, an ambience of earth browns and forest greens and antler-shaped chandeliers.

"Will she get off?"

"Well, her choices were sound. Her diagnosis was correct. I think, yes. She let maintenance know about the problem, and requested a gate be installed."

"Maintenance was told."

"Officially, yes."

Simon nodded.

"Then you're all after the wrong people. How did she become the defendant?"

"Personally, I think she rocked some boats. She petitioned for some changes at Helsey and won. She made the wrong people mad and they're getting back at her. Officially, the charges are that she could have restricted her patient's free access to the premises."

"Just playing devil's advocate," Henry put in.

"Absolutely. I think it's preposterous."

"It's certainly unfair."

"But it's more than that, Henry. You can't do for one patient what you're not prepared to do for all of them."

"Every inmate at Helsey."

"We don't like to call them that, Henry."

"You'd have to give each one—"

"Not each of them, but certainly every one with a similar condition."

"What's the percentage of those, Simon?"

"Roughly—I'd only be guessing. About ten percent."

"All at various stages of the disease. Some worse, farther along?"

"Some with a later stage of the illness."

"Who weren't any more safe or unsafe with access to the same areas inside the building, or outside of it."

"Oh. Yes, I see where you're going." Simon grinned a warm, infectious grin. "You're a damned good attorney, Henry. I'm awfully glad you're around."

Simon felt better, thanks to his friend. His strategy would take on a new approach. Henry's reasoning was sound. He'd apply it to the case.

When both men were satisfied and happy, they retired to the bar and surrendered to the ministrations of Alice. She served them hefty tumblers of brandy, stoked the fire, and propped the downy pillows thrown across the couch that faced the hearth. She told them that the bar would close, but that they could stay until the wee hours, as the fire would last and their rooms were right at the head of the stairs.

When the men did finally climb the stairs, the lodge was quiet. The heavy wooden steps creaked and groaned, and they found themselves whispering.

"I'll see you in the morning," Henry muttered. "Sleep in," he added, then slipped into his room.

Simon's den was glowing with a fire. It warmed the wooden beams and floorboards so that the room felt like a sauna. He cranked the casement windows open, then stripped off his clothes and crawled onto the bed. He'd fought fatigue all night, but couldn't shortchange Henry. So he fell into the strong deep currents of sleep, and forgot the things that troubled him.

Chapter 15

WHEN MORNING BROKE, it was the chime of church bells that woke Simon. He reluctantly lifted himself onto his elbows and thought longingly about staying in the bed he'd slept in. It had the smoothest sheets and the softest pillow he'd ever known. Henry was an early riser. One look at the clock told Simon that his friend would no doubt be downstairs having his second cup of coffee. Still he lay there, not wanting to leave the warmth and comfort of the bed. Only one small thing in the world could improve this oasis…he pictured Martha, and imagined her slim frame tucked up in the hollow of his arm.

He turned on the radio, and the strains of an old familiar song flooded the room. Maybe it was the alcohol, the nostalgic talk with Henry—but Simon couldn't catch his breath. His hands trembled as he went to the sink. He ducked his head under cold running water, dousing his hair and his neck. He remembered the song, and how she always loved it. *All right*, he thought. *You've allowed yourself the sweet memories.* He snapped off the radio.

Henry waited down by the water in faded denim jeans, sitting on a deep wooden chair with wide slats, his feet thrust into loafers. His white cotton shirt was rolled up at the sleeves. He turned and grinned at the sight of his chum.

"Glad I could take you up on the offer of a room." Simon gratefully accepted a steaming mug from Alice, who then retreated up the stone path to the main building.

Henry motioned for Simon to sit, then looked after her.

"Nice woman, that Alice. I'd like somebody like that at home with me."

Simon looked back over his shoulder. "Maybe she's unattached. Do you want me to put in a good word for you?"

"No, no," Henry said pensively. "I'm devoted to the single life. Aren't you?"

Simon couldn't honestly say that he was. Not now. Not anymore.

"Look out there," Henry pointed east. "Loons. They've been singing for the past half-hour. They live in this whole part of the country, right up into Canada. Just the right terrain, with the lakes and whatnot. Still, it's sort of a haunting sound."

"Yes. It is." Simon looked out across the water at the black-rimmed fowl. He listened to hear the sounds of his own unease.

"…wills, trusts, and estates," Henry was saying. "That's all I've been hearing for the last three months or so. I'm setting something up for an elderly client I've known all my life. Makes me feel good to be of some help now."

"Sounds interesting," Simon said politely.

"So many people, on the verge of bankruptcy. You know how the story goes. A fellow loses his job, or hits some unforeseen snag. He has lots of personal expenses. The first thing he knows, he's fleeing creditors.

"You see, Simon, you mustn't look at it from a narrow medical view. You're focusing in on the patient and her immediate condition. But if you entertain the more far-reaching aspects, you can see what a catastrophic event it is for the survivors. If none other than from a financial aspect? Take Henning, for instance."

"I don't like this guy, Henry. I don't trust him."

"Which, I hate to say, has much more to do with your feelings for Martha than anything else."

"All right. I admit I care about Martha, but that just isn't it, Henry."

"I'm being too harsh."

"Not that… Explain what you mean by cata-strophic," Simon said. "I mean, once the sick person is shut away, I'd think the spouse would have a field day from the unburdening."

"Dear man, you mustn't forget that someone has to pay the bill. And with a disease like that, it's a doubly cruel fate. The person you knew is gone, but you're still paying those bills. Unless there's a trust in place far enough in advance. But as you well know, you just can't plan those things."

"Hmm?" Simon asked absently.

"Take Martha and Mrs. Henning. She died of Alzheimer's?"

"She suffered from it, but she died from massive amounts of water filling her airways."

"Right. And you need to train the spotlight on the guilty parties."

"We need to find them first. I don't like to see any-body blamed for this thing. You know, much as I hate to say it, unfortunate things happen sometimes. I'd almost have to say, the more I hear about the setup, that it was more a matter of security—breach of security—than any-thing else."

"Has Martha been allowed to continue on staff in the interim?"

"Oh, yes. I made sure of that. I mean, this isn't like a surgeon who's considered dangerous to his patients. She's competent. She's just—"

"What?"

"Young, I guess," Simon said. "Not jaded enough to have cut off Grace Henning from what was probably the only thing left in her life that brought the woman any pleasure."

"Sounds mildly condescending."

"Not at all. It's more of an indictment of myself. I would have taken care of Grace. If it was up to me, she wouldn't have half of the freedoms Martha gave her."

"Then Martha was too lenient?" Henry asked.

"Martha was just fine. Grace was lucky to have had somebody like her."

"Tell me, about how long did this Mrs. Henning suffer?"

"We're not sure exactly, it's such a sneaky disease," Simon said. "Maybe for some time. Who knows?"

"Well, how long was she institutionalized?"

"You can't go by that, Henry. I mean, sometimes you don't even know until it's long underway."

"And her survivors?"

"Her husband."

"Tough break. Did he—?"

"Why all the questions?"

"You have to forgive me," Henry said. "I'm an attorney. I think like an attorney. Liabilities and assets. It's about all I get to think about."

"What did you say?"

"Just wondering if they'd written a trust, that's all. It takes a few years to establish before it kicks in. Otherwise, there's no protection—"

"For the assets," Simon muttered.

"What say?"

"Assets and liabilities." Simon stared out at the loons, and his voice dropped to a whisper. "So, he'd lose a fortune if Grace were to linger too long."

"Meaning?"

Simon bolted from his chair. "Henry, I'll be in touch." He sprinted the path to his jeep, gunned the engine, and tore out of the parking lot, pebbles flying, tires burning. He gripped the wheel hard in his hands. His palms were wet, his forehead bathed in a cold sweat.

*

Martha Reed phoned John Henning from home to set the record straight. She'd tell him she was flattered by his invitation, and that she had enjoyed herself. She would say that anything other than a casual, friendly relationship between them was out of the question. He would understand. He'd have to.

But Henning wasn't at home. The phone rang several times and Martha ended up leaving a message, asking him to come by the office, that she would be there all day. There were no patients coming in on a Sunday. The office would be quiet. Thank God. Yesterday, she'd told Simon the whole story. But that did little to kill the feelings of guilt and of doubt.

When she arrived mid-morning, she was still battling her conscience, and took a walk around the parklands that bordered the sanitarium, trying desperately to sort things out. Once she'd laid a single foot along the path, her mission was compulsory. It seemed only natural to visit Grace's private sanctuary.

She picked her way carefully along the trail, as Grace and she had done before. The two women had been like school children on a stolen holiday. They had shared a sense of adventure and took incidental pleasure at each new turn in the trail. Today there was no gladness in the path she took. Martha knew where it would lead, but without Grace, the joy was gone, and she wondered if she might not just turn back.

Ten minutes was all it took, from the back door of the Institute to the precipice of the cliff, where ice cold water churned and frothed below, and the sight of the overflow brought a stinging rush and a breathlessness to anyone lucky enough to witness it.

Martha was seconds from the cliff, heard the gurgling water around the bend, smelled the heavy moisture on the air current coming from up ahead.

A golden wash covered everything.

She took careful steps down a small detour to the base of the falls. She slipped off her shoes and slid in, wading just to below her knees, holding her cotton skirt up high, just out of the water. It was not something she'd have done on a regular working day, but today was Sunday, a day of rest.

The water numbed her toes and ankles and worked its magic up the calves of her legs. It was the soothing cold of a liquid icepack. She hopped up onto the rocks, legs dangling from the edge, and closed her eyes.

She thought of better times, and considered the visits Grace may have had by herself to the refuge. What a peaceful mecca. Martha was mesmerized by the magic of the water, the opulent landscape.

She spent the better part of an hour there, judging from the direction of the sun. Afternoon was approaching. Reluctantly she dragged herself up, knowing a pile of paperwork lay on her desk. She had to get to it today. Tomorrow Helsey would hum with the stuff of an ordinary business day, and there would be no time.

It was almost enough—this idyllic setting, the backdrop of the falls—to make her forget her troubles, and the accident. The case would wind up soon, within the next few weeks. She could think of nothing she had done other than to be the best caretaker she could. She had loved Grace in her own way, and would look to the future with a clear conscience.

Simon's insinuations about her and John Henning were hard to bear. It had been one night's dinner. She had gone as much to console John—and out of curiosity—than anything else. She mused that maybe Simon only made it an issue to elicit a reaction. What to do with Simon? She'd have to reexamine any sentiments she harbored. Last night they'd been at each other's throats. An outsider would never guess they were two people who profoundly respected one another, let alone had other, more personal feelings.

He was always a valiant guardian, never needing showy signs of material wealth to bolster who he was or what he stood for. He never groveled for anyone. Always sure, steadfast in his belief, in his foresight. Why wouldn't she trust him? Simon filled her head as she stepped out of the cool spa and up onto the footpath, donned the soft leather shoes she discarded earlier, and picked a leisurely path back to Helsey.

*

Not a moment later, she stopped, short. Surely her eyes deceived her. The article lay ten feet ahead, to the right of the footpath, snagged on a thorn bush. Afraid to touch it, she did so with a tentative hand, half expecting it to vaporize.

A small piece of cloth, an almost insignificant size, caught between the thorns. The world in a microcosm. Martha pulled at the silky shred with the small silver ball at its end. It trickled into her palm. And suddenly, what it was and what it meant dawned on her, so suddenly that she dropped it, recoiling. In that instant, she knew what Grace had suffered.

There had been no hallucinations, though they fit so neatly with the diagnosis. She had never looked beyond the obvious. And Grace, the hapless creature who saw through the mime, wasn't taken seriously. While Martha insisted it was all in Grace's mind, Grace had somehow, after all, been pursued by a villain made of flesh and blood. And all the while she had been lucid. Grace had been right when she said she'd never be taken seriously.

Martha retrieved the condemning evidence from the grass and held the silky piece of purple cloth. She shook it, and the swatch came to life in the merry tinkling of a single bell. How appropriate that she be the one to find it. It tore her conscience to bloody shreds.

She clutched her stomach, fighting a loathing that burned inside. Nausea crushed her, until she lay on her side, staring blankly at the cloth, rubbing it between her fingers, refusing its message. She rolled over and heaved into the bushes. Her stomach purged, she pushed the cloth into her pocket and rubbed a sweaty hand along her thigh. She ordered herself to concentrate and drew deep, ragged breaths to keep from passing out.

Martha struggled to her feet, gathered her skirt, and limped back toward the building. She grazed the corridor walls, swaying off balance, and rattled the door handle she had left unlocked, entering her office.

With shaking hands, she searched for the light switch on the wall. She crossed the length of the room, collapsed in her chair, grabbed for the phone. She couldn't wait to tell Simon. If he agreed with her findings, she'd go to the police with the evidence. The phone rang until the voice mail picked up and she heard the first few words of his message.

"Where could he be?" She bit her lip until it bled. After the beep, she said, "Simon, when you get this, come to Helsey. It's urgent." Her hands trembled uncontrollably as she dropped the receiver back onto its cradle.

She busied herself with distracted, unproductive movements: shuffling papers, tearing open envelopes she couldn't force herself to read. The anxious, scattered thoughts combined with fleeting glimpses of her dreams of Grace's face full of fear, pleading and imploring. They made no sense, and Martha hoped that Simon might help sort things out. This idea consumed her, so that she saw him as the savior from her grief.

Tension pounded at her temples. Blood rushed to her face in waves of heat. Suddenly the room was too small. She grabbed the corner of the desk and doubled over. She had to get back outside. She lurched around the desk and almost didn't hear the office door creaking wide. John Henning stepped into the office.

"John!" She swallowed hard. "I'm so glad you're here."

"What is it?"

"I found something. I don't know what it means, but I think Grace was right. There's more going on or—more that went on. Oh, I know I'm not making any sense, but—"

How could she tell him what she couldn't understand? "I can't breathe in here. It's stifling. My stomach's queasy."

"It's all right," he assured her, and put an arm around her waist.

"I was sick. I—" she finished lamely.

"It's okay. There's nothing to worry about. Let's get you a little fresh air." He led her out into the corridor and down the dimly lit hall. "How long have you been here?"

"I don't know." She heaved and fought to hold back the churning in her stomach. "Get me outside. Hurry."

*

Martha and John navigated the path along the outskirts of Helsey. John encouraged her to place one foot in front of the other.

"All you need, I think, is a bit of fresh air," he said.

"Yes." She nodded, trying desperately to clear her head.

"It's a glorious day, isn't it? Just perfect for a little walkabout, hmm?"

John's arm around her was firm and strong. It was the support she needed.

"I want to—I need to talk," she blurted. She had to confide in him, and reason it out.

John halted in the path and turned to her, holding her hands in his own.

"You haven't—lost your job at the clinic?"

"No, nothing like that. But it's worse."

"What could be worse than that?"

Martha bowed her head and shook it. She reached into her pocket and pulled out the bell. "There were no hallucinations," she said, and looked up at a wide-eyed and silent John.

He reached out wordlessly, and took her by the arms. There was an intensity as he pulled her closer. "Martha. Darling."

He pinned her deeply with blue, blue eyes, and Martha witnessed a strange suspicion she'd never noticed before. Emotion passed over his features like clouds whisking across the sky, casting the day in shadows. There was disappointment. And regret. And then, she saw resolve.

Seconds stretched into moments. John's gaze fixed her. She took an instinctive step backwards, felt his arm around her waist. He pulled her up directly to look into her face, and he asked, "Would you like to see the waterfall? It's very pleasant there."

Chapter 16

SIMON RACED DOWN the mountain, reviewing how he'd put it all together. How long did Martha say Grace had been showing signs? It seemed from the records that her deterioration was rapid. Maybe not so rapid. What if she'd been unwell for a very long time and no one noticed, or did anything about it?

Quite by accident, Henry had triggered his suspicions. He wasn't sure until now. John Henning was a smooth operator, all right. And dangerous—oh, so dangerous. Simon took the hairpin curves down the mountain. Martha wasn't answering her cell. "Dear God," he pleaded as the jeep hugged the ribbon of pavement, twisting and swaying. "Don't let him near her."

*

The man of charm had been replaced by a demon: eyes glittering, fingers clutching her arms to the point of pain. There was a wild, untamed look in his eyes, and all of her background and training seemed to desert her at the time when she needed it most. She tried to muster some semblance of clear-headedness, to explain the things instantly unfolding. John lowered her onto a rock at the edge of the bluff. She couldn't help but look up.

"Why did you call me?" she asked. "What did you hope to gain?"

"I wanted to see you. I was beginning to like you, actually."

"That's bullshit, and you know it. You wanted something. What was it, information?"

"No, not at first," he said. "At the start I thought you'd make an interesting companion. I quite enjoyed the single night we had together. And there would have been many more if it hadn't been for the damned investigation. When they began digging around, looking to blame someone, I knew it was time to back off. At the same time, keeping in contact with you would give me a chance to know how the investigation was going. After you'd been cleared, who knows what might have been?"

"You expect me to believe you really cared for me?"

"Oh, as much as I've cared for anyone, I suppose." He hissed into her ear, "You should never have come back here. What is it they say? One must never go in search of trouble, because you just—might—find it."

"How did you do it?"

"Planning. To fail to plan is a plan to fail, my dear."

"How did you get to Grace—?"

"In New Orleans? Simple. I just went off to Royal Street, that's all. Those antiques I'd bought with Jack had to be shipped. I just decided to add one last item that I couldn't quite decide on earlier. And that gave me the half an hour I needed to perform for my lovely wife in the garden."

Martha stole a glance behind him. There was the slight possibility that she could make a run for it, if she caught him off guard. But how?

"Why?" She focused again on the face of a stranger.

"Did I kill her? You're assuming that I have killed her. It's always unwise to make assumptions. But then, you know that, don't you? You've learned from experience."

"How long was she sick?" Martha had to know.

"Oh, I'd been covering for her for a very long time. It wasn't fun anymore. After the incident with Louise Gladley, there was no hiding it. I thought she'd go quickly after that. I'd kept her out as long as I could, sheltered what assets there were."

"How did you get around the fence?"

A glistening stare. "That was an imaginative piece of work, if I say so myself."

"I had it fixed. I was afraid she'd go there alone."

"Actually, you did me a favor when you requested the gate. Oh, I'm sure you had visions of being able to share this place with the other 'inmates' and it made things so much easier for me. Grace loved it here." John looked around and smiled. "She didn't break her promise to you, really. She never came here alone. But she went with her harlequin!"

"The gate was secure."

"Even a secure gate can be left open."

"Who—?"

"Your Mr. Greeley, I'm afraid."

"Greeley. He's the one who called to say she was missing!"

"He was the one who should know."

Martha nipped at her lower lip, inching away, as he leaned back casually against a jagged wall.

"You're a bright woman, Martha. I'd say if anything though, you're too trusting. You see the good in people. You're blinded to the rest."

"You said Greeley was involved."

"Dear girl, it's naive to think there's anyone, anywhere who can't be bought."

An image of Simon Talbot flashed through Martha's head.

"It's too bad. If only you hadn't gone looking…I'd have had my money, Grace would rest in peace, and you and I—that's the terrible tragedy, Martha—you and I would drift into the sunset. You should have seen her face that night of the bonfire. You were all crouched around the flames with that ridiculous old man telling his story. Grace was so out of it, she never questioned the fact that I was there one minute, and gone the next. Right about the time that harlequin came calling."

"She saw you at the bonfire?"

"And then promptly forgot."

"I never saw you."

"My dear, I was always in costume."

It all made sense now. Her mistake had been becoming emotionally involved with Grace. It had clouded her judgment, and unintentionally contributed to the Grace's demise. She had assumed her patient was the only one who knew about the waterfall.

He'd taken her to the grotto. What was once a heavenly place, was now the scene of nightmares come true. Martha looked down at the water below. John's arms held her, inching her toward the edge.

Martha peered up across his towering form. Oddly, she registered his faultless appearance, his stunning appeal. A perfect physical specimen of a man. The devil himself, assuming the form of an archangel.

"I thought you were a happy couple," Martha said, stalling for time.

"We were. Why do you assume mine were all bad intentions?"

"You killed her."

"I put her out of her misery. They do that much for the horses at Saratoga when they fall and break their legs!

Exquisite creatures, blighted beyond their capacity to be used and enjoyed."

"Is that how you saw Grace?"

"Grace was a trophy wife, yes. She looked good on my arm. And I quite enjoyed being married to her—and she to me, I might add."

"You used her illness. It was a tool for you, to exploit her."

"I took the thing that invaded our lives, and I used it to good advantage." He tossed his head to the side. "That's all in the past. Let me tell you something. Men of fortune look ahead; foolish ones look behind. The past is dead, my dear Martha. And so is Grace. May she rest in peace."

With that, he brought her up to him, close, within inches of his face. He cupped his hands around her buttocks and pressed his pelvis into her own. Martha stepped backwards and away, but the maneuver only positioned her against the rocks. He pinned her there, looking down almost tenderly at her face while a small smile played across his lips. He toyed with her, amused.

"You pig," she spat.

John grabbed her forearms and forced her mouth to meet his own, then broke away a fraction of an inch from her face, as she fought to get away.

He's going to kill me. Martha squinted at her opponent. She'd have to fight him for the prize. Life, or death. She brought a powerful knee up to his groin as quick and hard as she could. He bent over and clutched himself between the legs.

"Jesus, you bitch." He straightened, with effort and a painful smile, renewing his grip. "That's it, fight me, Martha. Go ahead. Give it all you've got, because when you're through, I'm going to have you. Right here."

He cast aside the smooth deceit and stepped forward, hands marauding over her. She knew she'd be no match for him, never have the strength, though she had the will, not only for herself, but for Grace. If this was how it was to end, so be it. But he was right. She wouldn't go down without a fight. She uttered the prayer that came to mind in clips and pieces. "The Lord is my Shepherd; I shall not want. He maketh me to lie down in green pastures. He leadeth me beside the still waters."

His composure changed to one of maniacal joy and promise. Did he relish the things he was about to do?

"He restoreth my soul."

John pushed her down to the damp grass, with a sneer and a smile.

Martha continued her litany through it all. "He leadeth me in the paths of righteousness for His Name's sake."

The last picture in her mind was the perfect, beautiful mask of a man who once intrigued her. He pulled at her blouse, licensed now to take his last advantage. She felt cold, hard ground beneath her, and heard the rushing water just below, hurrying to its distant end. She squeezed her eyes shut, and wondered if Grace had felt this lonely at that last moment, when there was no one but this twisted, wretched man. His hands came up around her throat.

"This is your fault, darling. Don't you forget. Your fault." He tightened his fingers. All breath escaped her, and she looked to the sky, eyes searching, struggling back to the prayer.

"Though I walk through the valley—of the shadow of death, I will fear no evil. For Thou—art with me."

A split second before the world was gone, a shattering blast brought her back, open-eyed, to see the mask crumple and shatter. John Henning careened over her. He slid through the mud and off the side of the ledge, grasping, screaming pitifully, and fell headlong to the water.

She catapulted to her feet, dazed and confused, casting around for some meaning. She could not look down into the swirling pool. She searched along the path, and scanned the farthermost point of the bank.

There, on a distant precipice, Simon Talbot stood holding a gun.

Chaptero 17

"MARTHA? Are you awake?"
"Do I look like I'm awake?" She was as pale as the sheet covering her, stretched supine on a hospital bed, trying to salvage decorum.

Simon bent over her. "Mm, well, your eyes are open."

"Then I'm awake."

"Sassy little thing, aren't you? You know I brought you flowers." He held out a large bouquet.

"Red roses!"

"I can take them back. If you're not nice to me."

Martha smiled, despite the tender bruises on her face.

"The doctor says you're going to be okay," he said.

"What do the doctors know?" she asked.

Her heart leapt at his lopsided grin; a weary foot soldier. She made an effort to sit up, took the flowers and grasped his hand.

"Simon, thank you. For the flowers and for—" the words caught in her throat "—everything."

"No, no, no. You just be quiet. Get your rest. The doctors are right; they're God, remember?"

"But, you—"

"Killed a man, yes. The world's most harmless man, himself a murderer."

"Nobody is calling you that."

"No. True. Only me." Simon sat on the bed alongside her, leaning over to kiss her forehead.

"You saved my life. What you did was the bravest, most..."

"Selfish thing," he said.

"No. How can you say that?"

"Because it wasn't you I was saving. It was me. I knew my life was ending, too." He reached a careful arm around her, avoiding the cuts and the bandages.

"I knew that my love for you was all there was left in the world that mattered." He snuggled her closer, and breathed into her ear. "Sleep now." He carefully laid her back onto the pillow, got up, and headed for the door.

"Simon, where are you going?"

"I'll be back. In a little while."

"Promise?"

"There's something I have to do at the office. Right now I want you to get some sleep."

He turned on his heel and left. Martha settled peacefully back onto her pillow.

*

Simon breezed past Nancy Ryan, who looked up from her keyboard, fingers suspended.

"She's fine," he blurted. "She'll be her old self in a few days." He disappeared into his office and fished through boxes at the foot of his closet.

"Nancy, where is that watercolor Mrs. Kelley gave me? The one of the leprechaun and the rainbow."

"Well, I think it's in there somewhere in the back. I thought you hated that painting."

"Ugly as sin," he grumbled as he pulled the item out of a cardboard box. "But it isn't nice not to appreciate a gift, and Mrs. Kelley is a lovely woman. Artistically challenged, but lovely, nonetheless." He strode over to the fabulous oil of sinking ships and ripped it off the wall.

"Dr. Talbot!"

"This depressing thing has got to go. Time to replace it," he said, hanging the garish picture, "with something more optimistic."

About the Author

Virginia DeMasi fell in love with Gothic romances at ten years old when she read *Rebecca*. She fell in love with the Adirondacks thanks to frequent visits to her uncle on Lake George.

DeMasi is a graduate of the University of North Carolina, Chapel Hill where she studied dramatic art and playwriting. After studying at the Institute of Children's Literature, she hosted *Storytime*, a weekly radio show on which she read and discussed classic fairy tales.

She has worked as a writer/producer of radio drama for the blind, and is co-producer of *La Familia*, a radio drama of ethnic Italian American heritage.

She lives in Hobe Sound, Florida.